WILD HUNT

SHADOW GUILD: WOLF QUEEN BOOK 2

LINSEY HALL

For my readers.

1

Eve

It was time.

I stared out the window at the full moon, counting the seconds past two a.m.

I'd been trapped in this damned tower for two days, locked in here by Lachlan, the shifters' alpha.

And my mate.

I could feel him even now, our bond pulling at me like an invisible wire through the ether. *I* sure as hell didn't want him, but fate felt differently.

Ha.

My life had definitely taken an insane turn for the worse lately. But we were about to put it on track. My friends and I had an escape plan in place, and it was meant to go down at two a.m. They were out there somewhere, ready to create a distraction, while I waited in my prison for my familiar to come break me out.

I searched the courtyard from my window, finally spotting a tiny shadow at the edge of the open, grassy space.

Ralph.

My familiar.

He ran in front of the shops on the other side of the grass. I lost sight of him, but he appeared on my windowsill a few minutes later, chubby and twinkly eyed. In his little paw, he clasped a vial of potion.

"You're late," I said.

He grinned toothily. *But I'm here.*

"Thank you. You are the best. And I mean that."

And don't you forget it.

"Now hand it over."

He raised his eyebrows. *Payment first.*

"You know I don't have any candy bars in here."

He scoffed, looking around me as if he might see a massive pile of them.

"When I'm out, you'll have your pick."

Satisfied, he nodded and pushed the vial of potion through the enchantment that protected the window, wincing when his little paw touched the magical barrier. It was meant to repel the living, but not the inanimate.

I took the vial and raised it, removing the tiny piece of paper that had been tied to it and unfolding it to read the spell written inside. My friends and I had gotten it from the witches' guild last night, and it was the answer to breaking out of here. Usually I could whip up some potions myself, but they took time to brew.

This had been quicker, and I wasn't willing to wait around for Lachlan anymore. I'd helped him catch a murderer, and his repayment was to lock me in this room. True, he'd just found out that I was his long-lost mate and that an insane killer was after me, but it was still too heavy handed.

Ralph turned and looked out at the courtyard. *The distraction should go off any minute.*

I smiled, grateful for my friends. It was late enough that I should be able to sneak across the roof unnoticed. But just in case, my friends were setting off a distraction on the other side of the courtyard.

Finally, I heard the little explosion and saw a poof of green light rise from the far side of the tower.

They did it!

Probably Mac, given her love of blowing things up.

"You should step aside," I said.

Ralph nodded. *I'll be waiting for you on the roof to show you the way down.*

"Thanks." I shivered at the idea of having to climb down the wall myself. Normally, I'd have my Fae wings. But Lachlan had taken my enchanted charm from me, and I was back to being a failed shifter without a beast.

So I would be getting down from the tower the hard way.

Ralph disappeared and opened the vial, sprinkling the glittering powder on the windowsill in front of the iron bars. It sparkled a pale blue, and I smiled.

This had to work.

Carefully, I pronounced the words on the paper. They were written in a language I didn't understand, but the witches had said it would be easy.

When the powder in front of me ignited, sending massive blue flames shooting upward, I grinned. They sparkled and danced, consuming the iron bars and the magical shield that keep me in here. The spell was silent, and the guards outside in the hall would have no idea what was going on.

Finally, the shield and the bars were gone. I could feel the absence of the magic. It had pricked at my skin whenever I had stood too close to the window, but now there was nothing.

Tentatively, I held my hand out toward the window. It went right through without pain or resistance.

"Hot damn." I climbed onto the windowsill, grateful there was no molten metal on the sill. The flame had devoured it all. Thank fates I was still wearing my jeans and boots.

Without a backward glance, I climbed out onto the tower wall. The stones were rough and uneven, providing plenty of handholds.

All the same, I was still six stories above the court-yard, and my stomach pitched violently. Damn, that sucked. I'd had no problem with heights when I'd had wings.

Psst!

I turned to see Ralph gesturing from a little ledge beneath the roof.

This way. We can go over the roof and down the side of the tower near the graveyard. No one will see us.

I nodded and followed him, clinging to the wall as my heartbeat thundered in my chest. When I climbed onto the roof, my heart rate calmed a little.

This was better.

Together, we crept silently under the moonlight, making our way to the side of the stone tower. The view over Guild City was magnificent in the moonlight, the ancient buildings all clustered together as winding streets cut through. The Shifters' Guild tower was tall, giving me a view of the other towers evenly located along the city wall.

It was magnificent, my home.

Would I have to leave it now that Lachlan knew who I was?

No.

I couldn't bear it. I'd barely managed to stay away the first time. And now I had a guild. True friends. No way would I leave them.

Hurry up.

Ralph's voice dragged me back, and I sped up. He reached the side of the building and began to climb down, graceful despite his bulk and tiny paws.

Awkwardly, I followed, my skin iced with fear.

What I wouldn't give to have my wings.

I'll get them back.

First stop on my journey tonight was my secret workshop, where I'd create the potion to enchant another charm that would make me Fae.

Halfway down the tower, I almost slipped. My heart leapt into my throat, and I scrambled to get another hand hold. As I hung there by my fingertips, cold sweat dripped down my back.

You've got this.

"Thanks, Ralph," I whimpered, clinging for dear life.

My toes found a foothold and I started again, slowly making my way to the ground. I slipped only one more time, but finally made it. The feel of the grass beneath my feet made my heart finally settle back in its proper place in my chest.

"I'm never doing that again," I muttered.

Come on. Ralph gestured me forward, and I followed, even though I knew the way. He had senses I didn't and knew his way around town like the back of his paw. True, his knowledge was mostly focused around where the best bins were located, but he still knew where he was going.

Together, we cut through the silent graveyard and out into the main part of the city, sticking to the alleys.

Finally, we reached a crossroads. I could go to the Shadow Guild tower where I lived or to my secret workshop. Ralph headed toward the tower.

"I'm going this way," I whispered at his back.

He turned, confusion on his little face. *Why? Our friends are meeting us at the tower.*

"My secret workshop is this way. It's where I make the potion that makes me fae."

Ralph frowned. *You're going to keep that up?*

I nodded. "Of course. It's part of my identity now."

And it should lesson the feeling of the mate bond that pulled at me when the necklace was gone. I didn't want to feel the bond. Even now, I felt the connection to Lachlan. And it was weird because I didn't actually like him. I was attracted to him, yes. But I didn't *like* him.

Fate didn't care about that. It wanted to smash us together, like a child playing with action figures and say, "Now kisssss."

Just because we *had* kissed, and it had been annoyingly phenomenal, didn't mean that my rational brain wanted to choose that. I'd fight it with everything I had.

Anyway, fate couldn't make you love another. It could just force you into proximity and make you want each other. The love had to happen on its own, and it was *so* not happening with Lachlan. Especially since fate also decreed that I would die when I finally succumbed to the bond.

So yeah, no. Not for me, thanks.

Fine. Ralph scampered toward me. *I'll come with.*

"Thanks, pal."

Together, we hurried through the silent streets of Guild City. I texted my friends to let them know I'd be a bit late, and we arrived at my secret workshop a few minutes later. I'd created the secret space to hide all my most valuable ingredients and to have a quiet place to make the potion that changed my species. Until recently, none had known where it was located except me.

The alley that accessed the tiny top floor flat was narrow and silent. I let us in through the little wooden door and climbed the steps to the top level. Quickly, I disabled the enchantment that protected the door and slipped inside, Ralph behind me.

He went right to the lamp on the side table and rifled around under the shade. When he pulled out a chocolate bar that had been taped there, he grinned.

"You'd better share," I said.

He grumbled and broke off half, then handed the smaller bit to me.

I scarfed it down while going to the worktable that was cluttered with ingredients. Instinct took over as I made the potion, chopping and grinding the ingredients until they were a fine powder. Within minutes, I had my little cauldron bubbling over a magical flame that I'd made on the wooden table.

It's quick to make?

I nodded at Ralph. "Fortunately, yes. It's just the ingredients that are hard to come by. And I have all of those."

Within twenty minutes, I had the potion made. It bubbled purple and bright inside the tiny cauldron as I searched for a piece of jewelry to enchant. The potion was too powerful to drink, but it worked if I dipped a piece of jewelry in it and wore it.

I found a silver charm necklace in a bowl at the back of the table. I kept a few things like that lying around, since several potions worked the same way.

Quickly, I dunked the necklace in the potion and watched as the glowing purple potion soaked into the metal. When it looked normal again, I put it on. Immediately, magic washed over me. I felt my ears tingle and new power fill my soul.

"Ah, that's better."

Ralph eyed my ears. *You look normal again.*

I nodded, grateful. But what was normal for me?

I was supposed to be a wolf, originally named Verity, but I didn't have a beast inside me. Was being a fake fae the real me? My adopted name Eve was certainly my real name now.

I shook the thoughts away. "Let's get out of here."

We left the flat, then made our way silently across

town, sticking to the quieter streets. When we reached the courtyard in front of the Shadow Guild tower, relief rushed through me.

Home.

The windows of the tall stone tower blazed with light, and red rose vines crawled up the sides.

As if they sensed me, my friends piled out of the main door.

"About time!" Carrow said.

"Thanks, guys." I grinned and hurried toward them.

We shared a group hug and stepped inside the tower. The main room of our tower was cozy and bright with a massive hearth that flickered brilliantly, and comfy furniture scattered at the edges. There were only six of us in the guild, and everyone was here tonight. Carrow—our leader—as well as Mac, Beatrix, Seraphia, and Quinn.

All of us misfits, all of us friends.

"Well, did everything go off without a hitch?" Carrow asked.

I nodded. "Thanks to you guys."

Carrow's gaze fell to the collar. "That's still a problem though."

I touched it, grimacing. "No kidding."

Lachlan could track me through this collar, and I needed it gone. "I'm going to head upstairs and see if I can find something in one of my potion books about getting it off."

"We're coming with," Mac said. "And you can update us about what's going on."

I nodded, grateful.

"I'm going to get pizzas," Quinn said. "And beer."

"You're the best." I smiled at him.

Together, we climbed the stairs to my workshop.

2

Lachlan

I stood at the cell door, staring inside.

My brother.

He ignored the bed that had been placed inside the cell and slumped against the stone wall.

Alive.

How was it possible?

"Stop looking at me like that," Garreth said, his black eyes flashing.

The whites were entirely gone, evidence of the Dark Moon curse that had overtaken his mind. All wolves were susceptible to it, but my line particularly so. Strong emotion made us vulnerable to the curse, and when it finally took hold, it sunk its claws into our minds and settled in deep, bringing out any darkness that lingered there. It emphasized all the bad while suppressing the good.

The worst part was that it stole a wolf's loyalty.

Once you fell to it, you were forever changed.

No longer loyal to friends. Family. Pack.

It would be better to be dead.

The question was...*how* had Garreth succumbed? I'd *seen* him die. Buried his body. And yet he was here.

Reanimation was not part of the curse.

After so long away, he'd returned to our lives, trying to erase his past. He'd killed two of his old friends and tried to kill me. Tried to kill Eve.

When we'd captured him, he'd confessed that someone else was out there, coming for her.

"Why her?" I asked Garreth. "Why is this person coming for her? *Who* are they?"

He just stared at me, eyes blank and cold.

"Tell me, Garreth."

Nothing.

We needed answers, but we'd have to find them another way, because Garreth hadn't spoken since he'd been under the influence of Eve's truth potion.

She was still locked up in the bedroom high in the tower. I needed to let her out, but it was the safest place for her right now.

My mate.

I couldn't believe it, but I could feel it.

And yet I had no idea what to do about it.

When Garreth had taken the charm that had hidden her from me, I'd felt it like a lightning bolt to the chest.

Suddenly, I wasn't alone anymore.

My mate was nearby.

It had been the most powerful, surreal feeling. Something I'd avoided my entire life, and yet it was here.

Even now, I could feel it. That connection binding us through the ether. A presence that aligned with mine somehow.

Finally, I wasn't alone.

No.

It wasn't possible. That feeling had to be false. *All* feelings had to be false, as long as I took the potion that the blood sorceress Mordaca had made for me. It suppressed emotion. Or at least, it had. Lately, it hadn't been working as well.

I reached for the flask and swigged back a big gulp of the potion-laced whiskey, watching my brother.

He was all the evidence I needed, confirming my determination to maintain my distance and keep things the way they were. I couldn't afford to feel for her. Couldn't afford to feel for anyone. Being alone—being cold—was the only way that I could protect my pack. From myself.

My pack was the only thing that mattered. My responsibility to them.

But then it happened, and I felt it.

The bond with Eve broke.

One second it was there, a light in the darkness of my soul. The next, it was gone.

I frowned, stiffening. What the hell had just happened?

Garreth blinked, looking at me with sudden interest. "What happened?"

"She's gone." Confusion flickered, then fear.

Had she been killed?

No.

I turned and ran.

Eve

An hour later, after updating my friends on everything that had happened and searching every book in my collection, it was obvious.

"I'm not going to be able to get this damned thing off by myself." I pulled at the golden collar.

Carrow approached, peering at it. "It can only be removed by the original maker?"

"Yep." I grimaced. "Mordaca. Blood sorceress extraordinaire."

Her name was printed on the back in tiny letters. It

had taken a potion to reveal them, and at least I'd been capable of making that.

"How the hell are we going to get her help?" Seraphia asked. "Isn't she like super famous and hard to get to? *And* she lives all the way across the world."

Mac was right. Mordaca lived in Magic's Bend, Oregon, which was way too far away.

"I have a transport charm," Carrow said.

"Me too," Mac said. "They'll get us there and back."

I turned to them, my heart feeling like it was going to burst. "Thank you, guys. I don't know what I'd do without you."

"Your weekends would be a lot more boring," Mac said.

"True."

Carrow looked over at Quinn, Seraphia, and Beatrix. "You guys good to hold down the fort?"

Quinn saluted. "I have the early shift at the Hound anyway."

The others nodded.

"Good. We'll be back as soon as we can." Carrow gestured for me to come closer. Mac and I joined her, and she chucked the transport charm to the ground.

A silver cloud poofed up, and I gripped her hand. Mac took Carrow's other hand, and we stepped inside the cloud. The ether sucked us through space, spinning us wildly until it spat us out on a quiet street in the middle of Darklane, the Dark Magic district where

Mordaca lived. It was early evening here, and though the sun still hadn't set, Darklane was gloomy and shadowed.

It was normal for this part of Magic's Bend, the dark magic district. The old Victorian buildings were covered in black grime, almost like soot, residue of the dark magic used here. Not all dark magic was inherently evil —it was all about how you used it. Most of what Mordaca did was above board.

I hoped that getting this collar off fell into that category.

"Come on." Mac pointed to a building a few doors down.

The old Victorian houses were pressed right up against each other, sharing walls in many cases.

The Apothecary's Jungle, Mordaca's shop, had once been purple. I could see hints of it through the black soot that now covered it from roof to base. We climbed the steps to the door, the sign on the front of the building creaking in the breeze.

I knocked, heart pounding.

A few moments later, it swung open.

Just my luck, it was Mordaca. She wore a plunging black gown with a thigh high slit, along with a massive sweep of dark eye makeup and an ebony bouffant hair style that would do Elvira proud.

She leaned against the door and tapped her pointed black nails against her arm, pursing her blood red lips.

Her gaze ran up and down my form. "You're not a real fae, despite those pointed ears."

"I'm not."

In addition to being a blood sorceress, Mordaca was an Unseelie fae queen. She'd be good at recognizing one of her species.

"That must make you Eve," she said. "I've heard of you. What brings you to my door?"

"Recognize this?" I pointed to the collar, and her gaze fell to it.

She frowned. "One of mine?"

I nodded.

"Lachlan. Why did he put it on you?"

"He thought I killed someone."

"Did you?"

"Not that person. And now he knows I'm innocent. We caught the killer. So it needs to come off."

"He has the key."

Irritation fluttered in my chest. "He won't take it off."

"Why not, if you're innocent?"

I debated how much truth to tell. "Because, apparently, I'm his mate."

Her eyebrows flew toward her hairline. "You don't say."

"And I don't want to be."

Her scarlet lips twisted. "Hmm. Poor form, Lachlan." She turned and gestured for us to follow her inside. "Come on in."

"You'll help me?"

She looked back over her shoulder. "Solidarity, sister. It was one thing for him to use it when he thought you were a murderer. It's another thing all together for him to keep a girl trapped because he might want her."

"He doesn't want me." The words popped out on instinct.

"The collar says otherwise." Her lips twisted again. "But that's *not* what I made it for. I won't have my magic used to trap another woman into something like that."

"Thank you."

She nodded. "It's only partially for you. It's more so I can sleep at night."

And that was why Mordaca's dark magic wasn't evil. She had ethics. She used blood in her work, which was definitely shady at times, but everything she did had a backbone of honor to it.

"Will it be hard to get off?" Carrow asked.

"Hard? No. Expensive? Yes."

"Expensive?" Mac frowned. "Why is it going to be expensive if you're doing this because he shouldn't have collared her?"

Mordaca laughed. "I'm not a saint. At least I'm taking it off. My willingness is because Lachlan shouldn't be using it that way. But I don't work for free."

"It's okay," I said. "I have money." The blackmail money that I'd never given Danny was going to come in handy after all.

"Good. We'll arrange payment, and then I'll get you out of that thing." She turned back around, waving a hand over her shoulder to get us to follow.

We trailed after her down the dark hallway. It was papered in black velvet wallpaper decorated with ornate flowers.

The workshop at the back of the house was of moderate size, but it was well stocked, with shelves lining all the walls.

Mordaca turned to me and we arranged for payment, then she got to work. "This won't take long."

I watched as she measured out the ingredients, adding them to a tiny cauldron that burned over a magical flame on the table. Everything she did was almost identical to the way I worked, until the last step

She held her hand over the cauldron and pricked her fingertip, letting a drop of blood fall into the vessel. It gleamed black and bright, and I'd never have the guts to ask why her blood wasn't red.

None of my business.

Finally, it was done.

"Come here." She waved me over.

I approached, stopping right in front of her. She dipped a paintbrush into the potion, then applied the liquid to the collar.

"So, are you the reason that Lachlan wanted to increase the dosage of the potion that suppresses his feelings?"

My gaze flashed to hers. "What?"

"I'll take that as a yes."

He'd increased the dosage? Did that mean he was beginning to feel despite the potion she'd given him?

Crap. That couldn't be good.

"Don't you have client confidentiality or something?" I asked her, wondering why she'd told me about that.

"Do I look like a doctor or lawyer?"

"No."

"Exactly." She painted more potion on the collar. "Almost done here."

The collar around my neck heated to an almost painful temperature before finally snapping off.

Relief flashed through me as it tumbled to the ground.

Oh, thank fates. I rubbed my neck. "Thank you so much."

Mordaca nodded. "Of course. I'll await payment later today."

"You'll have it."

We said our goodbyes and left.

As we stepped onto the main street, I spotted Lachlan. He stood on the other side of the road, staring at us. Confusion flickered on his face, replaced by understanding.

"Let's go." I grabbed Mac's hand.

She plunged her hand into her pocket and withdrew the transport charm. Quick as a flash, she chucked it to the ground. A cloud of silver smoke billowed up, and she took Carrow's hand.

Together, we stepped into the cloud, letting the ether suck us away.

When we landed in the courtyard of our tower, everything was silent for the briefest moment.

Then something small crashed against the ground at our feet—a potion bomb. I had barely a second to process what it was before it shot out a percussive blast that set Mac, Carrow, and me flying backward. I sailed through the air, crashing against the ground in a heap. My head hit a rock, and pain flared through me, making everything spin and my mind go blank.

"Eve!" Carrow's scream snapped me back to consciousness, and I sat up, frantically blinking to clear my vision.

A figure loomed in front of me, reaching down to grab me.

Lachlan.

But no. This man was even bigger, and he reeked of dark magic. I couldn't see his face through the shadows, nor as he gripped my arm and yanked me up.

In the distance, my friends screamed. I could see them beating at an invisible barrier. Somehow, this man had put a wall between us so they couldn't get to me.

I thrashed, kicking out as I reached for a potion vial in my cuff.

He dodged the kick but wasn't fast enough to get

away from the acid powder that I blew at him. He winced, stumbling backward as he let me go.

I turned and ran, but he grabbed my arm and yanked me back, pulling me against his hulking form.

"You're not going anywhere," he growled.

Fear iced my spine as I elbowed him in the gut, then stomped on his foot. Neither seemed to affect him, and he threw me over his shoulder, his arm an iron band over my legs.

Frantic, I reached into the ether, withdrawing a dagger that I'd stashed there using magic. I plunged it into his side. He flinched but didn't put me down.

Heart pounding, I withdrew the dagger and stabbed him again and again.

Magic exploded in the distance, and out of the corner of my eye, I caught sight of my friends hurling potion bombs at the barrier he'd created, trying to break through. I kept stabbing him with my dagger, no doubt making mincemeat of his internal organs, but he didn't so much as make a noise.

What the hell *was* he? A freaking zombie?

Desperate, I thrashed.

Finally, something seemed to impact him. He stopped, and I tumbled off his shoulder, hitting the ground hard.

I rolled aside, leaping up and raising my blade.

Lachlan, wild in his wolf form, leapt at the man. He was massive, his dark fur gleaming as his eyes blazed a brilliant green. He fought with such ferocity that it sent a chill down my spine.

He clamped his jaw on the man's shoulder and yanked.

The man, whose face was still shadowed—by magic, no doubt—stabbed Lachlan in the side, throwing him off.

Lachlan growled and leapt upright, dark blood dripping to the grass below him. He prowled between me and the kidnapper, lunging forward.

The man took one look at him and ran, spinning around and sprinting down the alley. Lachlan chased after him, and I followed, lungs aching as I tried to keep up.

Ahead of me, at the end of the alley, a burst of silver smoke appeared. The man lunged into it.

The little cloud dissipated before Lachlan reached it.

The alpha stopped, staring at the space where the man had disappeared. I swore I could feel his frustration vibrating the air.

Finally, he turned from it. With a swirl of green magic, he resumed his human form and strode toward me, green eyes flickering with worry and his jaw tight with anger.

"What were you doing?" he demanded.

"Fighting for my life." I glared at him. "What the hell did it look like?"

He stopped in front of me, only inches away. His

chest heaved with exertion and his eyes flashed as he looked down at me. In the shadows, he was as terrifying as he was beautiful. The strong lines of his face were almost brutal in their beauty, and the worry in his eyes slipped inside my soul and tried to warm me toward him.

I resisted, shoving it back. "Thank you," I said stiffly. "I appreciate your help."

I did. I was no dummy. Of course I did. That didn't mean I still wasn't pissed as hell at him.

"You shouldn't have left the tower." His voice was almost a growl.

"You locked me up."

"It was safe there."

"Maybe in your head. But not from the perspective of a prisoner, and you didn't explain what the hell was going on."

"Would that have made a difference?"

"Only if you did it while unlocking the cell door and letting me out."

He dragged a hand over his face, looking at me with dark eyes. His sigh was long and loud, as if he had no idea what to do with me.

Well, it didn't matter. Because he had no say over me.

Slowly, he reached toward my neck, hovering his hand an inch over my skin where the collar had once been. "You took it off."

For the briefest second, he didn't lower his hand. Though we didn't touch, tension sparked in the inch of air between our flesh. It warmed me, making my breath go short and my mind go slightly fuzzy.

It was almost like the alley had become a cocoon—just the two of us.

I shook off the damned fog of attraction. *Stupid fate.* Making me feel things I didn't want to. "Of course I took it off. Mordaca wasn't pleased with the reason you kept it on me."

"Bloody sorceress." He drew his hand back, then winced, pressing a hand to his side.

Concern streaked through me. I was mad at him, but what if the blade had punctured a vital organ? I wasn't heartless. "You should get that seen to."

"No offers of a healing potion?"

"I thought you didn't take them."

"I don't. But I do want to come back to your tower and discuss what the hell is going on."

I raised my brows at him. "That seems rather equitable of you. Are you sure you don't want to throw me over your shoulder and drag me back to *your* tower?"

"Honestly, that's exactly what I want to do. But you wouldn't stay put."

"And it's freaking barbaric."

He inclined his head just slightly, and I took it as agreement.

"Glad you agree." I looked him up and down. He'd

been the only one able to scare off my attacker, and he was also in possession of Garreth, the only clue in all this.

We had to work together. I liked it as much as a cat liked water, but it was necessary.

His gaze flicked to my ears. "You changed back."

"I did. It's who I am now."

"It's not even close."

I barely knew who I was as a shifter, and I'd spent all my adult life as a fae. "It's who I am."

With that, I turned and stalked down the alley. "You can come if you want."

He said nothing, but I heard the faint sound of his footsteps behind me.

He hadn't mentioned the fact that we were mates.

Why not?

Hell, perhaps I shouldn't look a gift horse in the mouth and just go with it. Maybe he wanted to ignore it as much as I did.

Doubtful.

We reached the mouth of the alley at the same time my friends did, nearly colliding. Carrow and Mac stumbled back, their worried gazes on us. Quinn, Beatrix, and Seraphia hurried up behind them.

I loved having all my friends here. The last week had been just me and Lachlan, and I liked the backup.

"The barrier just fell," Carrow said. "Are you all right?"

I nodded. "I'm fine. You?"

"Yeah, we weren't the one grabbed by a madman built like a redwood on steroids."

"Who was he?" Mac asked.

"I have no idea." I frowned, realizing that I'd never seen his face. Even when he'd stepped directly into the moonlight, it was like he'd been shrouded in shadow. Clever magic, that. "Let's go in and talk about it. Lachlan might have some ideas."

Carrow's blond eyebrows shot upward as she looked him up and down. Her gaze landed on the blood soaking through his shirt. "You should have that seen to."

"I heal quickly."

"From a stab wound?"

He nodded sharply.

"The alpha heals quicker than the rest of us," Quinn said, his gaze on Lachlan.

Quinn should be in Lachlan's guild. He *had* been, in fact. All the way up until the Shadow Guild had appeared, revealed after being hidden by magic for centuries. It had called to Quinn, the way it had called to the rest of us, and he'd left the shifters' guild to join us.

I'd never asked him why Lachlan had tolerated that.

"Let's go talk this out," Lachlan said.

3

Eve

The seven of us headed back across the courtyard to the tower, Carrow in the lead. Lachlan brought up the rear, and I could feel his alertness as he scanned the space all around, looking for threats.

"You'll have to increase your security," Lachlan said.

"We will." I had no idea how, but we'd find a way. There were only six of us, and we weren't a particularly wealthy guild. Broke, pretty much. But we were powerful, and Carrow's boyfriend was loaded. He'd want her protected. We'd manage.

Carrow led the way into the tower. The hearth blazed to life, the light gleaming on Cordelia and Ralph. They sat in front of the fireplace. Cordelia had a packet of Monster Munch in her paws, whereas Ralph held a massive chocolate bar.

It was the first time I'd seen the two raccoons together—they'd seemed to almost studiously ignore each other up until now—and they turned to look at us. Each clutched their snacks close to their chest.

"Are you doing a trade?" Carrow asked.

The two raccoons just glared and then scuttled off to the side of the room.

Carrow's eyebrows rose. "Seems to be private dealings."

I wished I could focus on raccoon drama right now. From the look in her eyes, Carrow wished it, too. She smiled at me. "This is your deal, Eve. You lead the meeting."

"Thanks." I appreciated the respect, though I *really* would prefer that this wasn't my deal right now. I turned to Lachlan. "Do you know who that was?"

"I've never seen him before. But he must be the one Garreth said was after you."

"Or a minion," Mac said.

I shivered. "I really hope there's not someone more powerful out there than him. He didn't even slow when I stabbed him in the back. A dozen times."

"Can a potion give him that kind of strength?" Carrow asked.

"It could, maybe. But I think we need to add that to

the list of mysteries." I looked back at Lachlan. "Why the hell is he coming after me?"

"That, I wish I knew. Garreth has said nothing more."

"There must be something special about you," Mac said. "Other than your potions and great hair, I mean."

"There's nothing special about me."

My friends laughed.

"*That* is not true," Mac said. "We just need to figure out what it is, then we'll know why he wants you. He wouldn't be after some random person."

"Maybe he's after Lachlan," I said. "That's what Garreth was after, right? He wanted to draw Lachlan to him, so he took me."

"That was a manifestation of the Dark Moon curse," Lachlan said. "Tearing apart your loyalties and making you attack those you once loved. This is different."

"Think, Eve," Carrow said. "Why would someone be after you?"

I chewed my lip. Damn it. Did I want to say it?

Was there any way to avoid it?

Not really.

And what did it matter at this point, anyway? I wasn't in the shifters' guild anymore, and I didn't want Lachlan to want me. Maybe it would help if he knew I was broken.

"I have no beast inside me, all right?" I said. "That's

one reason I pretend to be fae. I'm not even a proper shifter like the rest."

"No beast? That's not possible." Lachlan frowned. "Wait, is that why you never shifted as a teenager?"

"Exactly. When the time came when I was thirteen, nothing. Crickets. My beast had always been quiet within me. When I tried to shift at thirteen, I realized that it wasn't even there."

Lachlan scrubbed a hand over his face. "That's unheard of."

"I know." Even half-shifters could shift. I was the spitting image of my mother, and even though I'd never known my real father, she had *definitely* been a wolf. I should have been one, too.

So what the hell was wrong with me? "I don't know why that madman is after me if I'm broken."

"You're not broken," Carrow said. "It makes you special."

"But not in a good way."

"Yes, in a good way," Mac said. "Why the hell do you think you're in the Shadow Guild with the rest of us magnificent weirdos?"

She had a point. This place had called to me as soon as the spell had broken and it had appeared.

"You're special," Mac continued. "And that's why he's after you."

I frowned. "I have no idea how to find out what's wrong with me."

"*Why I'm special,*" Carrow said very slowly. "That's what you say now. *Why I'm special.*"

"Fine, whatever. But until I can figure out what my deal is, we should focus on the other things we know. Like Garreth. I can try to make more truth potions, but they'll take time to brew."

"If Garreth is just a minion, he might not know any more than he's already told us," Lachlan said.

I could understand why he wanted that to be the case. Better for Garreth to be brainwashed than evil.

But could there possibly be a cure for him? There was supposed to be no cure to the Dark moon curse, but maybe...

"What else do we know?" Carrow said. "Our starting points?"

"Garreth was supposedly resurrected for this," Lachlan said. "I put his body in the ground myself seven years ago."

"That's a good place to start," I said. "Whoever did that had major magic and would have had a serious reason. It could lead us to the attacker. Our only clues about him are the fact that he was huge and impervious to daggers. His guts should be bolognese by now, and he just kept going."

Lachlan nodded. "You're right. Garreth wasn't buried in the city, though. He wanted to be buried in the Highlands."

"So we go there," I said.

"Now?" Carrow asked. "What can we hope to find at a grave that is seven years old?"

"Can the sorceress help again?" I asked. She'd helped us see past actions at his father's grave.

Lachlan nodded. "Perhaps. I'll ask."

He turned away and made a call. We waited, anxious vibes filling the air. A moment later, he turned back to us. "Grave is too old to find much."

I nodded. "Okay, so we can't see exactly what happened at the grave. But I might have something that can reveal some clues. If we're lucky."

Lachlan nodded.

"I'll come with you." Carrow turned to the others. "You guys stay here and work on reinforcing the tower and our courtyard. Strangers already aren't permitted entrance without permission, but we could extend that to the courtyard with some other spells."

"On it," Seraphia said. "They won't know what hit them."

I let out a shuddery sigh of relief. We had a plan. The Shadow Guild could accomplish anything. Not without some blood loss, but thus far, we'd gotten a long way without casualties. Our streak would continue.

It had to.

"How long do you need, Eve?" Lachlan asked.

"Give me an hour. Then we can meet to go." I looked at Carrow "That good with you?"

She nodded. "Everything is good with me. I'm just backup."

"Thanks."

I didn't look at Lachlan as I turned and headed up the stairs to my workshop. I knew there were some potions that could reveal what spells had been performed on a place, so that would give us some clues. Not as good as getting a window into the past like the sorceress could do, but helpful.

I reached the room and found Ralph sprawled out on the windowsill, a bag of monster munch on his furry chest.

"So the deal went through?" I asked.

Yes. I still prefer chocolate.

"Well, it's good to try to expand your horizons." I wanted to grill him about Cordelia, but now wasn't the time.

There was time for a quick stress chocolate break, however. I retrieved a tiny bar that had been taped under the lip of a table, unwrapped it, and shoved it in my mouth.

Ralph sat bolt upright, eyes wide. *What did you do there?*

"Nothing." But my words were garbled.

He narrowed his eyes. *I'm watching you.*

"Trust me, I know." It was getting harder and harder to hide my stash from him now that he'd sort of moved in. "Keep eating your monster munch."

He shoved one into his mouth while maintaining eye contact, then laid back down.

Quickly, I set about making a truth potion. The ingredients were expensive and rare, but I had enough for three doses. I made sure they were boiling away on their cauldron. They'd take a while, and the flame was magical, so I could leave it brewing. That done, I set about gathering supplies, turning when I heard footsteps behind me.

Lachlan strolled in the door.

The breath left my body.

It was the first time we'd been truly alone, and the air grew thick with tension. Just standing near him felt like an embrace.

There was so much left unsaid between us...

None of which I wanted out in the open.

"Almost done." I turned away to keep working. "I'll be down soon."

"You're my mate."

"No, I'm not."

"Just because you have that necklace on, and I can't feel the bond, doesn't mean you aren't my mate. I know it's there."

"Well, I don't." *Lie.* "And it doesn't matter anyway. I want to choose my own fate. My own partner."

He nodded, his jaw tight, and something unrecognizable flashed in his eyes. "Fine."

"Fine?" Shock flashed through me. He was just going

to give up like that? Male shifters always aggressively pursued their mates. Generally, the females pursued them right back.

And he was just *fine*. He was going to let me go.

But of course he was.

He'd called me a mutt when he'd learned we were to be mates so many years ago. Old hurt welled to the surface. It didn't matter that it had been ten years and I looked different now. He still didn't want me.

Good. I ignored the hurt. It was insane that I should feel it. Because I didn't want him either. Even more important, our most revered seer had prophesied that our bond would lead to my death.

So yeah, I couldn't pursue anything there anyway. Didn't want to, and straight out couldn't.

"I'll meet you downstairs."

"Fine." He turned and left.

Fine. There was that word again. The dumbest, weakest word in the history of time, and he'd just used it twice.

There was more to *fine* than just fine, that was for sure.

But I didn't have the time—or the desire—to figure it out.

Lachlan

. . .

I strode down the stairs, unable to banish Eve's face from my mind.

Fine.

I was anything but fine. It had taken everything in me to stay on the other side of the room. Even though she wore the necklace that buried our bond, I could feel the faintest traces of it, and it made my head spin.

The hurt that had flashed in her green eyes when I'd said "fine" had burrowed a little hole into my heart, and it stung. Hurting her made my stomach turn.

No doubt she remembered my cruel words from so long ago.

I dragged a hand through my hair.

They'd been necessary, just like this was necessary. I couldn't let her influence me. My pack needed me.

There was only one thing keeping me from turning into Garreth, and that was my self-control. I could only maintain it if I kept my emotions entirely at bay. Mordaca's potion still worked, but less effectively every day.

Eve was too much of a risk. She could make me feel, and that would be the beginning of the end.

If I fell to the Dark Moon curse, I would do far worse than Garreth had. I was too powerful. Too strong. If the alpha turned against his pack, it would be catastrophe.

I'd had to put down my father for that very reason.

I clung to the memory, using it to harden me against

Eve. I couldn't ask my pack to do that. Watch me lose my mind and then be forced to kill me.

"You all right?" A voice dragged me out of my dark thoughts, and I realized that I'd reached the main room.

Carrow leaned against the wall near the fireplace, her gold hair gleaming under the light. A fat raccoon sat at her side, and I wondered what it was about this guild that attracted the strangest familiars.

"Yes."

"Don't look all right," she said. "Were you bothering Eve?"

"Yes."

Her eyebrows shot up. "Didn't expect you to admit it."

I shrugged. "It's clear enough that I'm a bother."

She looked me up and down, a thousand thoughts flashing in her eyes. I didn't want to know a single one.

When Eve clattered down the stairs behind me, I turned, grateful.

"Ready?"

"Ready." She nodded, her gaze moving to Carrow. "You?"

"Yeah. Let's go." Carrow pushed herself off the wall and went to the door.

We followed, Eve brushing past me to walk alongside her friend. My gaze lingered on her, unable to look away.

Damn it, this was going to be trouble.

Between the charm she wore and the potion I constantly drank to keep any emotions at bay, we had some help in this fight to ignore the bond. But still, it seemed insane that we would try.

No one ever resisted the bond. Not forever.

And the more I looked at her, the harder it seemed.

I reached for the flask and swigged back a healthy dose of the potion-laced whiskey.

Head in the game.

We just had to solve this problem, then I could go back to life as it had been. Comfortingly cold.

4

Eve

Carrow led us out into the courtyard, then looked at Lachlan. "Which way?"

"The cemetery near my tower."

She nodded, then turned and strode through town. I caught up to her, pressing close to her side. "Thanks for taking charge."

"You came downstairs looking like you'd been hit by a truck," she whispered. "Thought I'd give you time to get your balance."

"I don't know if I'll ever get my balance."

"Want to talk about it?"

I looked back at Lachlan, who followed ten feet behind us, giving us space. Or avoiding me. Hard to say.

"He knows I'm his mate." I swallowed hard. "And he seems determined to ignore it."

"That's a good thing, right?"

"Extremely good." My stupid, traitorous heart couldn't help but be a little bothered, particularly when I remembered his cruel words. I didn't want him, but it still hurt. "It's just so strange. Shifters never do that kind of thing. It's impossible for them."

"You said before that he drinks a potion that suppresses his emotions? Maybe that's it."

"Yeah." And the fact that he didn't like me. "I should make sure he always has that damned stuff available. Buy a keg, maybe." Though it seemed a terrible way to live.

I shot him another glance, unable to help myself. His powerful stride ate up the street, and his face was set in determined lines.

If Lachlan was one thing, it was determined. He was all duty and honor to the pack, and if he really was worried about the Dark Moon curse, then it was vital that we avoid each other. I could understand that, and it worked best for me.

I turned back to Carrow as we cut through the main part of town. The street was wide and open, the midday sun bright on the windows, making the diamond panes gleam like gems. The ancient facades of the brown and white buildings looked particularly pretty in this light, and I could see the tops of several guild towers rising in the distance.

I was struck again by my love for this place. There was nowhere else like it. Sure, my life would have been safer if I'd stayed away, but I couldn't bear to be anywhere else. Now that I'd found my home in the Shadow Guild, I knew why.

I just needed to figure out what the hell I was.

Not a proper shifter, not a true fae.

Just really good with potions.

Finally, we reached the shifters' turf. The grassy courtyard was empty despite the good weather, and we cut across, heading toward the cemetery. As we neared, both Carrow and I slowed, letting Lachlan take the lead.

When he was far enough ahead, Carrow leaned toward me. "There was a prophecy about me and Grey, you know. It didn't pan out the way everyone expected."

Grey had been her fated mate as well, though the specifics of the bond had been a bit different since he was a vampire, and she was a soulceress.

"Are you saying you think that Lachlan and I will somehow end up together?"

She looked at him, then shook her head. "No. He's too cold for you. But I'm just saying that prophecies can be tricky things, and it would probably be smart to learn more about yours."

"I'll put it on the list."

She was right. I needed to know more about what the hell was going on here.

Lachlan stopped in front of a massive old tree that towered toward the sky, its twisted branches tipped with bright green leaves. "This is a portal to the Highlands, our ancestral homeland."

"That explains your accent," Carrow said.

He nodded. "We spend a lot of time there, particularly as children. Then again when our beasts want to run."

My gaze dropped to his bloodied shirt. "Are you sure you're good to do this?"

"Nearly healed." He raised his shirt to show bloodied skin, but no wound. The ridges of his abdomen look brutal beneath the layer of blood, like he spent his life doing sit ups to avoid feeling anything.

Sounded boring.

Looked hot, though.

I moved my gaze away. "Let's go."

He nodded and turned, stepping through the gleaming portal. Carrow and I linked hands and stepped through.

The ether sucked us up and spun us through space, sending us careening wildly as my stomach lurched. It spat us out on soft green grass. Huge white clouds filled the blue sky, and sun gleamed brightly from between them.

All around, massive mountains soared. In the

distance, a river cut across the landscape. To my left, the stone circle rose proudly against the mountains. To my right, the ancient castle that served as the shifters' country home was as welcoming as I remembered it.

I sucked in the air, unable to banish the memories of playing in these hills as a child. Before I'd realized that I was so different, things had been good.

It had been too long since I'd returned here. I might not be a proper shifter, but this still felt like home.

"This way." Lachlan walked toward the castle, and we followed.

The cemetery was located right behind it, though we couldn't see it from here.

In the distance, I caught sight of several wolves running. Longing surged within me.

I wanted that. So badly.

Carrow gripped my hand, as if she knew.

"Thanks," I whispered.

"Things are going to get better, I promise. I was a weirdo, too, for the longest time. Still am, but I did eventually figure out *what* I am. You'll figure it out too."

"I sure hope so."

As we neared the castle, I caught sight of movement in the windows at the top. The building was similar to their tower back in Guild City—full of dining rooms and bedrooms and communal spaces for the shifters to hang out. Way more kids than back at Guild City and, therefore, usually a lot louder.

We cut around the side of the building, heading toward the cemetery in the valley below. Ancient oaks surrounded the headstones like sentries, guarding our ancestors.

A tiny cottage sat between the trees, smoke drifting from the chimney.

"Who lives there?" Carrow asked.

"Grounds keeper," I said. "I don't remember her well, but she was a little odd."

As we neared the cemetery, the door swung open and a tiny woman rushed out. She couldn't have been more than five feet tall with wild short hair and bright green eyes. She wore four dresses layered over each other and grinned widely at us.

"Are you here to visit, Alpha?"

I glanced at him, catching sight of the kind smile on his face. "Yes, Agnes."

She nodded, gesturing behind her to where four hedgehogs sat, tiny and fat. "The spirits have been busy, according to my companions."

"Can you see spirits?" Carrow asked.

"No, but they can." She pointed to each of the hedgehogs in turn. "John, Paul, Ringo, and George."

"Nice to meet you." Carrow nodded at the woman and the hedgehogs.

The woman nodded, and her gaze moved to me. Confusion flashed on her face. "Verity? Is that you?"

Verity.

The name my mother had given me. I hadn't heard it in so long that it made my heart jump. Even Lachlan hadn't used it.

Truth. My name meant truth, and I'd spent my whole life living a lie.

Nope. Not time to go down that path.

I had no idea how she'd recognized me. "It's me, Agnes. But I go by Eve, now."

"You disappeared. The spirits were all aflutter."

"Really?" I frowned. "That's weird."

"Very. Not the kind of gossip they are usually into."

An idea flashed "Have the spirits ever mentioned Garreth? Is he one of them?"

Agnes frowned, her gaze going to Lachlan. "Now that you mentioned it, I'm afraid to say that they never have. He's not one of them. Quite odd, that."

Not if he was still alive.

"Can we visit his grave?" Lachlan asked.

Agnes nodded. "Of course, go right in."

"Thank you." Lachlan headed toward the headstones that sat in the shadows of the oak trees.

We followed. When we were far enough away, Carrow leaned close. "She's not really the grounds keeper, is she?"

"Not as I recall. She's kind of an odd duck, and this is where she wanted to live."

"So Lachlan let her."

I shrugged. "Seems so."

"She should join us." Carrow smiled. "More than enough room."

"Agnes would never leave the Beatles or her spirits."

"No, good point. We certainly can't offer that."

Lachlan stopped in front of a simple grave with a sturdy headstone.

Garreth MacGregor.

He stared down at it, his brow creased.

I couldn't imagine burying a sibling—seeing the body—and then having that person walk back into my life.

So just what the hell had happened here?

I pulled my bag from the ether, hoping I could figure it out.

"What are you planning?" Lachlan asked.

"I have a potion that will reveal if a spell has been used here in the past. Depending on what type of spell, we might be able to see evidence of it." I pulled a vial of potion from my bag, along with a plastic spray bottle from the pound store.

I decanted the potion into the bottle, then screwed the cap on.

"Not very fancy, I know." I stepped up to the grave. "But it works."

As quickly as I could, I sprayed the liquid all over the ground surrounding the grave, trying to hit every blade of grass with my potion.

When I'd used up the last of it, I stepped back and shoved the spray bottle back into my bag.

"The second step is a powder," I said, pulling it out of my bag. The container was just large enough that I could fit my hand inside. I grabbed some of the sparkling white powder and began to sprinkle it over the grass.

As I worked, sections of grass began to glow. A large design appeared, intricate and beautiful lines that swept through each other.

"Is that a Celtic knot?" Carrow asked.

"I think so?" I tilted my head to look at it. The grave was located right in the middle. "I don't know what it means, but I'm sure someone does." I looked up at Lachlan. "Any guesses?"

He shook his head but withdrew a cell phone and snapped a picture. Quickly, he inspected it, frowning. "It doesn't show."

I reached into my bag for a small pad of paper and a pen, handing it to Carrow. "Can you draw it?"

"Sure." She took the supplies and got down to work.

I strode around the grave, examining it from all angles. This design was important, no doubt, but what about inside the grave? I looked up at Lachlan, not wanting to be the one to suggest it.

He stared down at the grave with his arms crossed and his jaw tight. "We need to dig it up, don't we?"

I nodded, glad he'd been willing to say it.

"I'll be right back." He strode off, and I watched him. Halfway to the castle, he reached into his back pocket and removed the flask, taking a swig.

"This can't be easy for him," Carrow said.

"No." I rubbed my arms, thinking of Garreth in the cell.

Crazed. Maybe not even real.

But if he was...

We had to find a way to cure him. Had to.

"Done." Carrow showed me the design. "Good enough?"

"Great. Can you send a picture of it to Seraphia? She can check her library."

Carrow nodded. "Good idea."

Lachlan returned a moment later with a shovel.

"If you have two, I can help," I said.

He shook his head. "I can do it."

He stopped next to the grave, staring down. "The thing is, when I buried him—not only did I see him, but I also *felt* him. It was my brother. The bond was still there, even after death."

"You mean it definitely wasn't a glamoured body?" I asked.

He nodded. "Exactly. It was him."

"So the guy in your castle is a fake?" Carrow asked.

"No." Lachlan shook his head emphatically. "He's not. He's definitely my brother. I can feel that, too. And he never had a twin."

I shivered as I looked down at the symbol written onto the grave. "Is this necromancer magic?"

Carrow studied it. "I've seen the symbol associated with a necromancer's work, and it wasn't like this. That doesn't rule it out, but I'm skeptical."

Lachlan frowned, his expression disturbed.

"We'll find out," I said.

He nodded and began to dig. I found a spot against the base of an oak, and Carrow joined me. "This is going to be a while. If you want to get out of here, it's no problem."

"I can stay."

"Thanks." I leaned against her as I watched Lachlan work. He dug steadily, his shirt soaking with sweat and his muscles straining with every movement of the shovel.

I wanted to offer to help again, but it was clear that he didn't want someone else digging up his brother's grave. Maybe it was some kind of weird penance thing, as if he felt guilty for living when Garreth had died.

Finally, his movements slowed, as if he'd reached the casket and didn't want to disturb it too much. Ten minutes later, he tossed the shovel aside and bent down into the grave.

Carrow and I stood, joining him.

I stared down in the dark pit, watching Lachlan lift the top off the casket. The wood was still in fairly good shape, but the body was largely decayed. Shifters didn't believe in the same preservatives that humans used.

"He's unrecognizable," Carrow whispered.

I wished he'd just been a skeleton—that would have been a lot more tolerable—but unfortunately there was more to him. Desiccated, thankfully, but still, it was disturbing to see someone you had once known in such a state.

"I don't recognize him," Lachlan said.

"Do you mind if I spray some more of my potion in there?" I asked.

He nodded. "I'll do it."

Quickly, I poured another bottle of potion into the bottle and tossed it down to him. He caught it and began to spray. When he was done, I sprinkled some more of the powder, careful not to get it on him.

The coffin began to glow with symbols.

I crouched down. "Do they look different?"

Lachlan inspected them, and Carrow joined me.

Finally, Lachlan said, "No. They all appear to be the same."

"Thank fates," Carrow said. "Because I'm not a great artist. I can make a plan of where the symbols are located on the casket, though."

"Thank you." I stared down at the body, debating. We couldn't tell if it really was Garreth, so there was one last thing we should probably do.

I just didn't want to have to say it.

As if she could read my mind, Carrow said. "I can take a sample of the body if you need me to."

Hero.

Lachlan's gaze flashed to her, shocked. Then his jaw tightened. "I'll do it."

Oh fates, it was just too much to have to be the one to disturb your brother's corpse. The fact that a version of Garreth was sitting in Lachlan's dungeons didn't make it that much better.

"I can do—"

He shook his head, cutting me off, then bent down and tore off a finger. My stomach lurched.

Damn, today sucked.

5

Eve

I watched as Lachlan replaced the top of his brother's casket and climbed out of the grave.

Quickly, I drew an empty potion vial from my bag in the ether. It was just big enough to hold the finger, and I figured it was better if Lachlan didn't have to hang onto it.

"Here, I can take that." I held up the wide-mouthed glass container.

He nodded, and I unscrewed the jar so he could put it inside. I screwed it up tight without looking at it. I did not have a strong stomach, and the stress of this made even chocolate bars unappealing.

"The witches can help us identify this," I said.

Lachlan nodded again and picked up the shovel, beginning to cover his brother's grave once more. I watched him, heart heavy. He shouldn't have to be alone for this.

"I can take it to them," Carrow said.

My gaze flicked between her and the land behind her. It was getting late—nearly four p.m., which wasn't late unless you'd missed your entire night's sleep—and I was exhausted. But I didn't want to leave Lachlan while he was doing such a tragic task. Not that I wanted anything else with him, but ditching him to do this dirty job while I ran off with the clue was just too ugly.

"Do you mind?" I asked.

"Of course not." She looked at Lachlan. "I can just go back through the portal, right?"

He nodded. "Just walk through. It will take you back."

"Great. I'll let you know what the witches say about this. And maybe Seraphia will have some clues about these symbols."

"Thank you, Carrow."

She smiled and squeezed my hand, then turned to walk back toward the portal.

I looked at Lachlan, wishing I could help but knowing the offer would be refused again. So I waited in silence, wondering what it must feel like to bury a sibling for the second time, especially when Garreth was sitting in the cell back at the shifters' tower.

The fact that he was, somehow, alive should be a good thing.

But was it?

Was he here to stay? Or was this some kind of temporary spell that brought him back to do something evil? The fact that he had the Dark Moon curse pointed in that direction.

Poor Lachlan couldn't even celebrate the fact that this brother was back—not when he'd come back the way he had. Not when he was a murderer. And not when he might disappear tragically if this was some kind of temporary magic.

Lachlan had been a dick to me when we'd been kids, but I couldn't help but feel for him now. Some people got the short end of the stick too often, it seemed.

True, Lachlan had been blessed with strength, power, looks, and intelligence. He was the damned alpha, for fates' sake. But as far as family was concerned...

That had been a bust for him.

For me too, funnily enough. What a crappy thing to have in common.

Finally, he finished the grave. The dark dirt was a scar next to the bright grass, and I frowned. "I can ask Seraphia to come here and fix up the grass nice. Maybe add some flowers."

His gaze flicked to mine, and for the briefest moment, I felt like I could see just a little more of him.

Gratitude flashed in his eyes, but it was gone so fast I thought I'd made it up.

"It's fine," he said. "Agnes will want to take care of it."

I nodded. "Sure."

Suddenly, exhaustion struck me, even worse than before. I hadn't slept in nearly forty hours, and it was just too much.

"Come on," Lachlan said. "You need to rest."

"I'm fine."

"You're not. You're dead on your feet."

I looked toward the portal, which seem so far away.

I don't want to leave.

I hadn't been back here in so long, and it was the place of my best memories as a kid. I wasn't quite ready to go.

"Come on," Lachlan said. "We'll get you a room in the castle here. It will be safe."

"I'll be fine in my tower." I could surely drag my tired arse back through that portal.

"I insist." There was something protective in the hardness of his voice, as if he hated seeing me tired.

The mate bond.

He shouldn't be feeling it—not as long as he took his potion, and I wore my charm. The two of us were so drugged up that the bond should feel miles away. And yet...

I shook my head.

Nah, crazy.

"I'll throw you over my shoulder if I have to," he said.

"I know." I gave up, following him to the castle. I wanted to get back inside there anyway, just to see it.

The structure was a massive stone thing, ancient and grand. The windows twinkled in the late afternoon sun, and the chimneys emitted pale gray smoke. I trudged up the wide stairs, following Lachlan through the massive wooden doors.

The grand entry hall was as welcoming as the shifters' tower in Guild City, done up in crimson and gold with comfortable furniture near the two hearths and massive wooden tables for meals.

An older woman hurried forward, her cheeks pink and her hair wild. "Alpha! We weren't expecting you. We don't have anything decent on for dinner."

"Anything will do, Marta." Lachlan smiled, and it was a kind smile. So strange to see that expression on his face, which I generally only saw when it was scowling or fighting. "Is the blue bedroom made up?"

Her eyes flared wide, and there was clearly something special about the blue bedroom. "It is indeed."

"Please bring food there for Eve."

"Thank you," I said.

Marta inclined her head. "Of course."

"This way." Lachlan didn't look at me as he led me up the stairs or as he led me into a gorgeous bedroom on the top floor. Huge windows overlooked the mountains beyond, and the furniture was a gleaming wood draped in blue silk. The massive bed looked so inviting I could weep.

I turned to Lachlan, who had stopped at the door.

"This is a nice room," I said.

"I don't want you out of my sight. And since you have gotten out of the collar, it seems I'll have to entice you rather than force you to stay near."

I looked back at the bed. "It's going to take more than that."

"Food will be here soon."

"That might do it." I met his gaze, and something passed between us. An electric current that was impossible to ignore. It lit the air with sparks and seemed to squeeze my heart.

His eyes darkened, and his jaw clenched. At his side, his fingers flexed.

He wanted to reach for his flask.

Did he feel something right now just standing here with me?

What the hell was happening?

I reached up for my charm, desperate to feel its comforting presence at my neck. Surely my spell was working. As long as I wore it, I was more fae than shifter. It should be repressing any kind of mate bond.

And yet, it was almost like we felt it now.

Lachlan made a low noise in his throat, shifting forward slightly. As if he wanted to walk toward me.

Instead, he spun on his heel. "I will see you in the morning."

He strode away, and I hurried to the door, watching him go. His powerful stride ate up the hall as he walked away, and as he turned the corner, I saw him reach for his pocket.

I slumped against the door frame, dragging my hand through my hair as my heart raced.

"Settle down, idiot," I said to the traitorous organ.

You settle down.

I jumped, turning to see Ralph sprawled on the huge bed. He was nestled amongst the pillows, a trash panda turned king.

"How long have you been there?" I asked.

Long enough to see it get all animal planet in here. The way he was looking at you... yowzer. Like he was a lion, and you were a gazelle. He was going to jump you right there. But mauling was not *on his mind.*

I grimaced, not wanting to discuss my non-existent sex life with a raccoon. A girl had her limits. "You have no idea what you're talking about."

Please. I've been around.

Yeah, I really didn't want to know.

None of your business.

"I didn't ask!"

You wanted to.

Oh fates. I wasn't going to survive this.

He sat upright. *Now, do you think they have the good*

stuff here? This place is fancy. *They must have the best chocolate.*

"I'm sure they do. And if you go hunting for it, you're going to be in big trouble."

Ha. As if they could catch me. I'm a master thief.

The memory of catching him in my underwear drawer flashed in my mind. He'd leapt across the bed and scampered down a tree, fat bum wiggling and tail waving. He was the least subtle thief in the history of time. "Sure, Ralph."

A knock sounded at the door, and Ralph perked up, nose twitching.

I turned, spotting the same older woman who had greeted us. Marta.

I didn't remember her from my childhood, but I'd stopped coming here when I was eight years old. Those years were fuzzy memories of playing in the hills with the other children.

"Dinner?" Marta held up the tray.

"Thank you so much."

She nodded and brought it to the table, setting it down gently. Then she gave me a long up and down. I stiffened, wondering if I was passing whatever test she had in mind.

"He doesn't bring women here," she said.

"It's not like that."

"Humph." She nodded. "Well, enjoy your dinner."

"Thank you." She left, and I watched her go,

reminded of the cook back in the tower in Guild City. What was it with these ladies? They were like protective mother hens over Lachlan when he could certainly take care of himself.

And *I* wasn't interested, anyway.

Then again, he was a well-loved alpha. And alone.

It was strange for a wolf of his age not to have found his mate. They probably worried about him.

Well, they'd have to keep right on worrying because I wasn't about to change that situation for him. And he'd made it clear he didn't want to go in that direction either.

Marta had barely disappeared when Ralph bounded off the bed and scrambled up onto the table. *Dibs.*

"On what?" I joined him.

All of it.

"You can't eat all of it." The spread was bigger than he was—steak pie, chips, veg, fruit, and a decadent looking slice of chocolate cake.

He reached out and dragged the chocolate cake closer to himself. *Dibs on this, then.*

"You're going to rot your teeth."

He gave me a fangy smile and reached for a handful of the cake, shoving it into his mouth.

I grimaced. "If you'd use a fork, we could at least share it."

He maintained eye contact as he grabbed another handful of cake from the other side of the slice.

"Right, that's clear then. All yours."

Ralph smiled and sat on his bum, picking up the plate and going to town on the cake.

I cut into the pie, setting aside a little piece for him, along with some chips and veg. "Eat this too, all right? You're going to have a sugar crash if you eat only cake."

But what a way to go.

I shook my head and began to eat, everything in me lighting up with joy at the taste of the food. Not only was I exhausted, but I was also famished. I couldn't believe I'd managed to stay on my feet so long, but adrenaline could do a hell of a lot when required.

Ralph begrudgingly ate his real dinner, perking up a bit at the chips.

"You have the palate of a child."

He shrugged. *So do you.*

I looked down at my plate, realizing I'd eaten all the chips, basically none of the veg, and I'd picked all the steak out of the pie. Damn it, the little bastard was right. And I should have fought him for some of that cake.

"I need to get some sleep." I stood.

Ralph looked out the window, his gaze skeptical. *It's still light out, granny.*

"Oh, granny yourself. Don't make any trouble while I'm asleep."

He put one paw on his chest, eyes wide. *Me?*

"Ha ha. I mean it."

He harrumphed, and I fell into bed. As I drifted off,

memories of Lachlan standing in the doorway flickered through my mind, the thought of his gaze making my skin prickle.

No. There was nothing there. There couldn't be. We'd seen to it.

6

Eve

It was the moon that woke me. The warmth on my face called to me, dragging me from my slumber.

Drowsy, I opened my eyes, spotting the full white orb hanging in the sky outside my window. I touched my cheek, marveling at the warmth of its rays.

I'd never felt anything like it. Warmer than the sun on a summer day.

And so...comforting.

I sat upright, gaze still on the moon. Drawn by it.

Next to me, Ralph lay on a pillow, snoring, a half-eaten chocolate bar still in his hand. I recognized it as one from my pocket but was too distracted by the moon to pay him any heed.

Almost in a trance, I walked toward the window, pushing it open. With the fresh air blowing across my face, the moon called to me even stronger. It was a siren call I couldn't resist, and I drew in a deep breath, reveling in the glow.

My soul felt full, my heart light.

Was this what proper shifters felt on a full moon night?

I tugged on my shoes and jacket. I hadn't taken off any of my other clothes, so I was fully attired.

Quickly, I hurried from the room, leaving a sleeping Ralph.

I felt in control of my actions—mostly. But there was something else—the call of the moon dragging me forward. I couldn't have fought it if I wanted to.

The castle was quiet as I crept through the massive wooden doors and down the steps. Out on the lawn, with the mountains soaring around me, the moon felt close enough to touch. I gazed up at it, enraptured.

In the distance, I caught sight of movement.

A wolf.

Massive, with gleaming black fur. He was so far away that I couldn't make out any details, but I knew it was Lachlan. He ran with powerful strides along the river, cutting toward the mountains.

Desperate desire filled me.

I want that.

Fates, how I wanted to be able to shift. It was an ache inside me.

Maybe I could.

This was so different, how I felt right now. The way the moon called. I'd never felt anything like it.

The stone circle in the distance caught my eye.

There.

It was a sacred place. If I were going to be able to shift, it would be there. I had to try. Memories of the failure when I'd been thirteen were pushed far to the back of my mind. I never thought of them. It had been terrible, the laughter of the other young wolves.

It didn't matter.

What mattered was the fact that I might be able to do it now.

I hurried to the stone circle, breaking into a run as I neared it. When I slipped between two of the towering stones, I felt the magic prickle over my skin.

Yes.

This would work. It had to.

With shaking hands, I removed my necklace, placing it in the grass at the edge of the circle. Immediately, I felt the surge of power as I changed, the fae magic dropping away so that my shifter self could return to the surface. The moon called even stronger in this form, and I could feel Lachlan.

Our bond flared to life, and I could sense him, miles

away. Running free. I was desperate to join him, a feeling that I needed to banish.

It was a crutch, that necklace. The potion Liora had taught me had saved me, but it was becoming a crutch.

I drew in a deep breath, feeling the pull of the moon overhead. It was so strong. I imagined becoming a wolf, my body and soul transforming. Joining with the beast inside me.

Yet, no matter how hard I tried, nothing happened. I felt the pull of the moon, but nothing happened

Frustration welled within me, followed by desperation.

No.

This was supposed to work.

I felt so different. The moon felt like it was part of me. Surely, I could shift.

I fell to my knees, grief tearing through me.

I thought I'd given up on this dream.

Warm tears rolled down my face.

Apparently, I hadn't.

I don't want to be broken.

A howl sounded in the distance.

Lachlan. So far away, from the sound of it.

Good. I didn't want him to see me like this. I rose on trembling legs, sucking in a deep breath.

I wouldn't let this get me down. I couldn't. It wasn't fair, but that was life.

Still, anger flickered.

I wanted answers, damn it. Why was I so different? What the hell was *wrong* with me?

I looked toward the center of the circle, where the stone basin sat. Dark stains marred the inside.

Blood.

There was one person who might know what was going on.

I scooped my necklace from the ground and put it back on, sighing in relief.

This is me.

And it was okay. I strode to the stone basin and drew a knife from the ether, dragging it across the heel of my palm so that red blood poured forth. It hit the stone basin, where it sizzled and smoked. Magic would determine if I were one of the pack, and if it did, the seer's cottage would appear.

But *would* it decide that I was one of them?

I'd left, but I'd been pack when I'd been born.

I crossed my fingers, hoping.

In the distance, near the river, a cottage shimmered into existence.

The seer.

I drew in a deep breath and left the stone circle, heart pounding. I needed answers. She would give them to me. She had to.

I walked across the grass, the moonlight pounding against my skin. Something thumped deep inside my chest, a knowledge that I didn't know how to interpret.

I searched for Lachlan in the hills, wondering if he realized I was out here.

Maybe.

Would he come close?

It was a moot point when I reached the seer's cottage. The door opened as I neared, and the older woman stared out at me, her gaze tranquil. Her long white hair trailed down her back, and her robe gleamed brilliant blue.

"It's very late for a visit," she said.

"Were you expecting me?"

"When I felt the moon, I thought perhaps."

"Can I come in?"

"I suppose you have questions?"

"I do."

She shook her head and clucked. "No one ever just comes for tea."

"That's because you hide your house unless we make a blood sacrifice."

She chuckled. "Fair enough. I'm not keen on company." She stepped back and gestured for me to enter. "Come in, then."

I followed her into the warm, cozy cottage. It was too...floofy for my taste, with a floral couch and ruffly pillows, but there was no questioning her power. It radiated out from her, filling the room with a slight vibration.

She turned to me. "Returned at long last."

"I left because of what you told me about my bond with the alpha." And because he'd been a bastard. "Of course it's been a long time."

"I thought you might do that."

"Wait, wasn't I supposed to? You said our bond would lead to my death."

She shrugged. "I'm not sure what you were supposed to do."

Frustration seethed through me. That was the thing about seers. They were immensely powerful, and what they saw was true. But they couldn't see everything. And that's where it got tricky.

"Why are you here?" she asked. "What do you want to know?"

"What the hell is wrong with me?"

Her gaze softened slightly. "Nothing, though I know you won't believe that."

"Of course I don't believe that. I'm a shifter who can't shift. The only one I've ever heard of." I gestured to the door and the stone circle that lay beyond. "I felt the moon *so* strongly tonight, and I tried to shift. Nothing. It's always nothing when I try." I heard my voice break and hated it.

"There is shifter blood inside you. And your father's blood as well."

"What was he? My mother never said. I assumed he was shifter, but maybe not."

"That, I do not know."

"Will I *ever* shift?"

She gestured for me to come forward. "Give me your hand."

I hurried forward and stuck my hand out. She gripped it with cold fingers, closing her eyes as her magic welled on the air. A moment later, she said, "You will shift. But into what, I have no idea."

"I'm supposed to be a wolf. My mother was a wolf."

"Perhaps you will be. But it isn't clear."

"It doesn't need to be clear. It's biology."

"We're not all biology, darling. We're magic, as well."

Damn it. Damn this seer and her vague information. "There's someone after me. Someone dangerous. Is it because I've got screwed up magic? Because I'm a weirdo?"

She frowned, as if she didn't like my phrasing, but only said, "Give me a moment."

I waited, impatience and desperation surging through me.

Finally, she said, "Yes. He is after you because of what you are."

I didn't like hearing it, but I wasn't surprised.

"And the curse of the mate bond? Does that still stand? Does Lachlan know?"

"I have not told him."

"That doesn't exactly answer my question."

"It's the best I can give you."

Damn. "Can't you tell me *anything* else about it?"

"I've told you all that I know about that. For now. But there is one more thing. Follow the moon."

"What does that mean?"

She gripped my hand harder, and magic sparked from her palm to mine, painful and bright. I yelped, trying to jerk my hand free. She let me go, and I looked at my palm.

A glowing circle shone there, about two inches across. Surprise flashed through me. "What's this?"

"Show me." Her voice sounded foggy, and there was something about her expression that was off. A haziness to her eyes and a slackness to her jaw. Her eyes widened with surprise when she saw my palm. "I've never seen anything like that before."

"But your touch gave it to me."

"It did?"

I nodded.

"It must be important then." She rubbed her head, wincing. "This is more magic than I'm used to using. You must go."

"But—"

"Go!"

"All right, all right."

She rushed me out the door, almost pushing me over the threshold. On the stairs, I turned back. "Thank you. If you think of anything else, will you—"

She slammed the door in my face.

I jerked backward.

Well, that was that.

Slightly shell-shocked, I stared down at my palm. The circle still glowed. So weird.

I shivered and turned to head toward the castle. It was nearly dawn, and the pull of the moon had lessened. It was almost like this horrible, magical, crazy night had never happened.

Except for the new mark on my palm.

I heaved out a breath and turned, striding back toward the castle. Despite the early hour, I'd gotten nearly ten hours of sleep.

When I reached the steps to the building, the huge wooden door opened to reveal Lachlan. He frowned at me. "What were you doing?"

I closed my hand into a fist, hiding the mark. "I went to the seer. Were you running?"

He nodded, and jealousy sliced me like a thin knife.

"Did the seer say anything useful?" he asked.

"No. I asked her why the killer was after me, and she didn't have much to say."

"Much? Does that mean she had something?"

"Not anything more than we knew."

"Hmm." His gaze moved over me, and suddenly, I felt like it was last night. Awareness pulsed in the air between us.

It was like I might as well be standing there naked. He kept his gaze above my shoulders, but I could almost feel it like a caress.

Fates, if this was going to haunt us all the time now, I was a goner.

What I really needed right now was for Ralph to come tearing out of the castle, an entire stolen chocolate cake strapped to his back.

Anything to create a distraction.

When my phone buzzed in my pocket, gratitude almost killed me.

I yanked it free and read the message. I looked up at Lachlan. "Carrow says that the witches are working on figuring out if that body part belongs to your brother, and if it's imbued with any dark magic. They need to see you."

He nodded. "And the symbols?"

"Seraphia hasn't found anything, but she thinks a woman named Nevaeh Cross might be able to help. She lives in Magic Side, Chicago."

"I'll go with you to see her."

"No." I almost shouted the word, then pulled back. *Whoa there, crazy.* "I'm fine on my own. And you need to go see the witches."

A shadow flickered across his face. "It's too dangerous for you to go alone."

He might not want to be my mate, but he couldn't fight that alpha protectiveness.

"I'll go with Carrow. You know how strong she is. And *I'm* strong. And we're going to Magic Side. The attacker will have no idea we're there."

He frowned, clearly not liking it. "It's not safe."

"And I'm not your prisoner." I turned and strode toward the portal that led back to Guild City.

I heard his footsteps pound down the stairs—unusual for him, the one who moved with the silence of a hunting wolf—and turned to look at him. "I'll fly away if I have to. Don't test me."

His jaw tightened.

I scowled. "You know as well as I do that neither one of us wants this bond, so you're going to have to tuck your wolf back inside and get it together."

His eyes flashed brilliantly green, as if the wolf were fighting to come out. His jaw tightened, and I watched him force the wolf back down.

"Exactly," I said. "We both have our reasons for avoiding this, and we need to remember them."

He turned and looked forward, but I caught sight of his fist clenching.

"There's something about you, Eve," he said, his voice a low rumble.

"I know."

The problem was, I didn't know exactly *what* it was about me.

At this point, I was worried that my attacker knew more about me than I did.

7

Lachlan

I escorted Eve back to guild City, having to force myself
to keep my eyes off her as we walked across the lawn.
She was even more beautiful in the dawn light, her pale
hair glowing brilliant silver and pink.

But that was only a small part of her allure.

Something was different about her.

I couldn't put my finger on it, but something had
changed.

If I'd wanted her before, it was even worse now.

Mordaca's damned potion was weakening every day
and being close to Eve was the problem.

It had been too much to take last night, the lure of

the mountains too great. Combined with the full moon, it had been impossible to keep my wolf at bay.

I'd given it free rein, taking to the mountains to run. The freedom had been glorious, until she'd come out of the castle. My wolf had scented her, going wild, wanting to be near her.

I'd kept control, keeping us to the shadows of the craggy cliffs, but it had been impossible not to think of her. Not to want her.

This kind of desire should be tamped down by Mordaca's potion. Hell, as long as Eve wore her fae charm, I shouldn't be able to feel it at all.

But when she'd taken it off last night, I'd nearly lost my mind.

I dragged a hand through my hair, unable to keep the frustration at bay.

What would I do when my potion wore off entirely?

No. Don't think of it.

I needed to focus on the task at hand. There was so much we needed to learn, and, as long as Eve's life was at stake, I needed to be at the top of my game.

Could I really let her go off with Carrow, alone?

I glanced at her, catching sight of the stubborn set of her jaw.

It looked like I was going to have to.

And I should. I needed to fight the mate bond, and this was a good way to start. Ignore the protectiveness.

Anyway, she was right. Carrow was powerful, and so

was Eve. I also couldn't afford to be with her any more than necessary, the way my control was fraying.

Locking her in my tower had been as dangerous for me as it was annoying for her. I'd been tempted to go to her every hour. Every minute. I still had no idea how I'd resisted.

And we needed answers fast. That meant dividing our efforts.

We reached the portal near the massive oak tree. "I'll go first."

If her attacker was waiting for her in Guild City, I wanted to be there before her. She waited while I strode through, an annoyed expression on her face.

The ether sucked me in and spun me through space, spitting me out in the early morning light of London. It was cloudier there and threatening rain, but when Eve arrived a few moments later, it was like she brought light with her.

Bloody hell, *brought light with her?*

What the hell was happening to me?

It was insane.

"I'm going to head over to my guild tower to meet Carrow," Eve said.

"I'll escort you."

"I'm fine on—"

"I'll escort you. Magic Side should be fine, as you said. But the attacker knows you live here."

Her jaw tightened, and she nodded. Together, we

walked through the city. The early morning rush had started, and the streets were full of supernaturals headed to work. Half of them clutched to-go cups of coffee and pastries, and we were halfway to her tower when Eve's stomach grumbled.

"For fates' sake, you need to eat more often. Come here." I gripped her arm and tugged her toward the coffee shop on my right.

"I don't need anything. Let me go."

"Just do this for me, all right?" It was downright uncomfortable the way I felt when I thought she might be hungry.

I knew I shouldn't care, just like I knew she wasn't starving. But just the *idea* that my mate might be the tiniest bit hungry...I couldn't take it.

My mate.

No. I couldn't think of her that way. It was deadly.

I focused on counting backward from one thousand, a trick I'd developed years ago to give myself a distraction from the misery of my father's and brother's deaths.

It worked. Mostly.

Within minutes, she had a sausage roll and a coffee, along with a supremely annoyed look on her face.

"There," I said. "Let's go."

She rolled her eyes, but bit into the pastry. Satisfaction rolled through me.

I started counting again.

We continued through town, reaching the Shadow

Guild tower ten minutes later. It was quiet in the early morning light, but as soon as we stepped into the courtyard, the door burst open and Carrow and Mac came flying out, followed by Seraphia, the librarian.

"Thank fates you're back," Carrow said. "Now get inside."

"Are you my escort?" Eve asked.

"No jokes, dummy. A crazy person is after you. Now shoo." Carrow made a sweeping motion with her hand, gesturing toward the door.

Eve hurried forward, and I followed. Carrow stepped in front of me, her eyebrows raised. She was of average height and build, with a wild mane of golden hair. Though her guild was small, her status was similar to mine in my own pack. She wore the responsibility with an easy confidence.

"She'll be fine," Carrow said.

Eve turned back to face us. "We've already settled on the plan, Lachlan. You see the witches; we'll see Neveah Cross."

"The witches need you to bring a sample of your brother's blood to them," Carrow said. "You're the only one who can do that."

She was right, damn it. "You'll transport directly to Magic Side from inside your tower? No cutting across town to get to the Haunted Hound to leave through human London?"

"Straight through," Carrow said.

I nodded, reluctant to leave Eve while the attacker was still out there, but knowing I had to. "Fine. Be careful. I'll come here when I'm done."

Eve nodded and turned back to the tower, entering without looking back.

Carrow gave me a long look, seeming to want to say something. Then she turned and left as well. Mac and Seraphia followed them in.

I departed, moving quickly across town, alert for anything out of the ordinary. The attacker wanted Eve, but he had something to do with my brother as well. He might be interested in me for that reason, and the last thing I needed was to be caught unawares on the street.

My guild tower courtyard was quiet as I crossed it and entered the tower. A dozen shifters were eating breakfast at the tables in the main hall, and I gave them a brief nod of greeting as I headed straight to the kitchens to get a small knife and glass vial for the blood sample that I'd need.

Properly equipped, I headed down to the dungeons.

Sick dread filled the pit of my stomach as I took the stairs two at a time.

My brother.

A miracle that he was back.

A nightmare that he was cursed. He'd murdered two of our pack members—two of his closest friends from childhood.

It didn't matter that he hadn't been in his right mind when he'd done it. They were still dead.

He was just a shell, now, and according to all of our legends, the Dark Moon curse was incurable. I'd had to put my father down when he'd gotten it, and it was likely only a matter of time before I'd have to do the same with Garreth.

The idea made me want to vomit.

When I reached the cell door, I nodded at the guards. Callum and Sophie were two of my best.

"How has he been?" I asked, hating that I had to keep him imprisoned but knowing it was the only place strong enough to hold him.

And how could I explain to the rest of the pack that I was letting a murderer go free? The alpha's family didn't get special consideration, especially when they'd committed murder.

"He's been quiet," Sophie said.

"Hasn't eaten," Callum added.

"Thank you. Take a break."

They nodded and strode from the hallway.

I stopped at the door and stared through the small window, watching my brother. He still hadn't moved to the bed—just sat on the stone floor, staring at me.

He looked so much like my father that it made my heart twist. His familiar features carried memories of better times, but those times were so far past that they might as well have happened to someone else.

"Hello, Garreth."

He frowned, almost as if he didn't recognize me. The idea that he might be having a hard time remembering me sent a thin blade into my heart.

I unlocked the door with the key that I kept in my pocket, then slipped inside and shut it behind me, locking it once more.

Garreth said nothing, just watched me.

"I'm trying to find out what happened to you, brother," I said. "So that I can cure you."

It was a secret hope that I'd hardly been able to hold in my heart. But impossible or not, I had to try.

"Can you tell me what happened when you died?" I asked. "Because your grave still has your body in it, and yet here you are. And you *really* feel like my brother."

He stared stonily. Silent.

"I'm going to need a blood sample from you for the witches." Would he fight me? I almost hoped he would. This stillness was eerie.

I removed the top from the vial and put it in my pocket, then knelt at his side, muscles tense.

He looked over at me as I reached for his arm. His eyes were pure black—not a hint of white.

Damned curse.

As soon as I touched him, his gaze cleared. The whites returned, and he blinked. "Lachlan?"

I felt like I'd been punched in the gut. "Garreth? Are you there?"

"What happened to you?" Garreth asked.

"What happened to me?" Hope flared in my chest.

This was my brother. This was *Garreth*.

"Nothing happened to me. But something happened to you. Do you remember? You're so different. So cold. And your aura seems broken. Flame and ice."

I blinked at him.

"You're different, Lachlan."

"I..." There was too much to say. *I had to kill our father when the Dark Moon curse took him. You have the Dark Moon curse as well.*

"You can't stay broken like this forever," Garreth said. "You're torn in two. It will eat you alive. Drive you mad. Like me." Garreth's eyes returned to black, the whites swallowed by ink. His face went slack again, and I felt my shoulders slump.

Damn it.

I'd never heard of a cursed wolf returning to sanity even for a moment, though.

Maybe we could help him.

Quickly, I sliced Garreth's thumb and took a small sample of his blood. He'd heal quickly, as I did. He didn't so much as twitch as the blade bit into his flesh.

It was worse than if he'd fought me.

When I was done, I stood.

"I'm going to help you, brother," I said. "We'll find a cure."

He said nothing, of course, and I left.

My mind spun with our encounter.

You're so different. His words echoed in my mind.

Was I?

Of course I was. The potion suppressed everything. But I hadn't thought others could notice.

I dragged a hand through my hair. *You can't stay broken like this forever. It will drive you mad. Like me.*

What the hell did that mean? Mordaca's potion was meant to suppress emotion so that I didn't fall to the Dark Moon curse.

If it also drove me mad, it would become a moot point.

What the hell did Garreth know, though?

Hell, it was all a mess.

I reached the Witches Guild tower on the other side of town and strode across the half-dead grass of their courtyard. Like all the other guilds in town, they had a tower that was set into the massive city wall. It sat opposite a curved row of shops, a courtyard in the middle.

Most of the shops were empty, given that shopkeepers didn't trust the witches. Their tower was chaos, an eternal party that never seemed to die. Spells went wild all the time, shooting from the chimney and windows, singeing the grass and the nearby buildings.

The Council of Guilds was supposed to maintain control of all guilds to keep the city operating smoothly, but they couldn't control the witches.

No one could.

Everything looked fairly calm this early in the morning, however.

As usual, the square wooden tower leaned slightly to the left, looking like a drunken witch with its pointed roof. The dark wooden stairs that wound around the outside of the building had a few pairs of women's underwear draped over the rails—everything from granny panties to lace thongs. Other than that, it all looked quiet.

I took the stairs two at a time to the door that was located halfway up the wall. Once there, I knocked.

A few seconds later, it creaked open. A dour butler stood on the other side, watching me with bland eyes. His black suit looked perfectly pressed, a contrast to the chaos in the house behind him.

"Who may I say is calling?" he asked.

"Lachlan. Alpha of the shifters."

He nodded, then turned.

"We heard!" A woman shrieked. "Let him in, Jeeves! We could use something nice to look at."

I couldn't help the small sigh that escaped, then stepped into the entryway. Jeeves led me back to a large room full of witches dressed like they were 1980s housewives. Shoulder pads, fitted skirts, neon heels, and massive hair. Each one clutched a champaign glass full of orange bubbling liquid as they sprawled on couches and chairs, all positioned around a table full of plastic boxes.

At the edges of the room, palm trees careened at odd angles, set into huge pots that had been decorated with tiny lights.

Three of the witches leapt to their feet and approached.

Coraline, Beth, and Mary were the leaders of the gang, temporarily in charge while their mistress, Hecate, was away. She'd been missing for one thousand years, though, so I was fairly certain it was permanent.

Coraline, her straight black hair streaked with green, grinned widely when she saw me. "Are you here for our Tupperware party?"

"Tupperware?"

Mary, pale, pink-haired, and dressed in a matching suit, held up a large plastic box. "It's important to have the right size. This is excellent for human heads, for example."

She beamed, not a hint of irony in her eyes. But maybe a little insanity.

"He's not here for the Tupperware party." Beth shook her head, sending her dark braids flying. "He's here for the spell."

"Ah." Coraline's eyebrows rose. "Of course. I got distracted by your pretty face."

"It's supposed to be a priority," I said, gesturing to the plastic boxes with a skeptical face.

"Hey, head storage is important," Mary said.

"It's fine," Coraline said. "The spell is almost ready to go, we just need your brother's blood."

"I have it."

"Then come on." She gestured for me to follow, then headed deeper into the house.

Mary and Beth joined us, and we went down several flights of rickety stairs to a large room in the basement. Dozens of tables were set up, each covered with vials of potions and smoking cauldrons. Spiderwebs hung in the corners, and a fat black cat glared at me from its perch on the closest table.

"Be nice, Satan," Mary said.

Satan hissed.

"Good boy," she cooed.

That was nice?

"This way," Beth gestured me over.

The table that I stopped in front of looked like all the rest—cluttered with supplies and potions, a single black cauldron burning over a magical purple flame.

"How much?" I pulled the glass vial from my pocket.

"A few drops will do," Coraline said. "Right in the cauldron."

I uncorked the container and let the blood drip into the cauldron. It sizzled and smoked. "Is that all?"

"For now. Give us a little time to finish brewing it, and we'll hopefully have some answers for you."

I nodded, turning to leave.

"You seem different," Beth said.

That was the second time I'd heard it today, and I didn't like the sound of it. "We hardly know each other."

She shrugged. "Doesn't mean I can't see that you're different. What changed?"

"Different, how? Be specific."

"Different than you were last month. More intense, or something."

Last month. That hadn't been what Garreth had meant. He'd known me ten years ago.

"What's different?" Coraline asked.

"Nothing."

"Not true." She grinned widely, tilting her head. "You're not as cold."

"I'm as cold." None of it made sense. Garreth said I'd turned cold; these witches said the opposite. Maybe they were both right. The years had turned me cold, and meeting Eve was starting to undo it.

Dangerous, was what it was.

8

Eve

Inside the Shadow Guild tower, I stood across from Mac, Carrow, and Seraphia, the hearth flickering merrily at our sides. Cordelia and Ralph were nowhere to be seen, and I couldn't help but wonder if they were together.

"As Carrow mentioned, I couldn't find anything about those symbols," Seraphia said. "But I have a friend who can help you. Carrow knows her, too."

"Neveah Cross," I said.

"Exactly," Carrow said. "In Magic Side. We'll go see her now."

I nodded, heart pounding, then stuck out my hand to my friends, holding it palm up to reveal the glowing white circle. I'd spent too long hiding before, and I wasn't going to do it anymore.

"Ever seen anything like this?" I asked. "Do you think it's like yours, Seraphia?"

She had a mark that glowed on her arm whenever she used her power—a brilliant vine that twisted its way up toward her shoulder.

Seraphia frowned. "Did it just appear?"

"Yep. Last night. I had this weird moment where I communed with the moon like an old hippie."

"Or a werewolf," Carrow said.

"Except I'm not one. Not really."

Carrow squeezed my arm, a silent gesture of support. "Whatever you are, we'll figure it out."

"Thank you. Truly." I looked back at Seraphia. "What about your mark?"

"I have to imagine it's a mark of power like mine, but no idea what kind. I'll look into that, too. Hopefully, I'll have more luck with that.

"Thank you."

"Let's get going," Carrow said. "It's still the middle of the night in Magic Side, and that's perfect for us. We'll be under the radar."

I nodded.

"Good luck," Mac said. "Just shout if you need help."

Carrow nodded, then reached for a transport charm in her pocket. She chucked it to the ground, and a silver cloud burst upward. We linked hands and stepped inside.

The ether sucked us in and spun us through space, spitting us out in the middle of Magic Side, Chicago. It was dark still, sometime around three a.m. The moon gleamed brightly overhead as cold wind whipped off Lake Michigan.

I pulled my jacket tighter around me. "Where is she meeting us?"

Carrow turned and pointed to the large stone building looming in front of us. It had a conical central dome and several colonnaded levels, a beautiful mish-mash of neo-classical and renaissance architecture that felt like a building out of time.

A moment later, a woman pushed open the large door and hurried down the monumental stairway.

She wore grey moto jeans and a brown leather jacket over a white silk shirt. Her red hair spilled over her shoulders, and she looked cool as hell.

"Hey, Carrow!" She stopped in front of us and hugged my friend, who hugged her back.

"Neve!" Carrow pulled back and gestured to me. "This is my friend, Eve. Thank you so much for agreeing to help us."

"Sure thing. Seraphia said it was important."

"It is, thank you." I shook her hand, and magic vibrated up my arm. She was powerful, but I couldn't put a finger on what she was. Seraphia hadn't known. "I really appreciate it."

"No problem. I'm kind of on administrative leave at the moment, so I've got plenty of time on my hands. I already gave Seraphia's notes to the imps. They're pulling some stuff out of collections."

"Imps?" I asked.

She nodded. "Most of our collections are stored deep in a pit that's been driven into Lake Michigan. You need wings to recover the books."

I felt my eyebrows rise. "Wow."

She nodded. "Yeah. There's an antique elevator. But its super slow, makes suspicious clanging noises, and drops precipitously from time to time. Imps are easier. Come on, I'll show you."

We followed her up the wide marble stairs to the entry, up some more stairs, then through a sky tunnel. Through the glass ceiling that arced overhead, I could see an enormous domed building rising tall.

We pushed through a pair of ornate doors and into the interior of the library. I whistled low under my breath. The place was utterly massive. In the center, an enormous circular pit dove hundreds of meters downward, bookshelves filling the space. Imps flew in and out, clutching books in their clawed hands.

"Welcome to the library." Neve gestured to the pit. "It's really easy to fall into a good book here."

"No kidding."

They had to have answers in a place this size.

"Come on." Neve gestured for us to follow, and we accompanied her to the edge of the pit, leaning over to see the bookshelves that spiraled down so far that I lost sight in the gloom. Neve's hair danced about the sides of her face as if there was a slight breeze- but the air was still. We made small talk until, a few minutes later, an imp shot straight for us.

"Here's our guy." Neve stepped backward, and we followed, narrowly avoiding a collision.

"They're fast when they're on a job," she whispered. "And they have terrible aim."

The imp grumbled. "You watch it, Neveah Cross."

Neve smiled. "Thank you, Brutus. You're my favorite, you know."

He scowled, but a blush spread across his face. "Be careful with these."

"Of course."

He handed off the books, and she led us to a table, taking a seat and passing a few to us. "These books contain any mention of the symbol you seek."

Carrow cracked her knuckles and put the original copy of her drawing in the middle of the table. "Let's get down to work."

I settled in with one of the volumes, leafing through as I searched for images that would match the ones in Carrow's drawing. After an hour, I'd still found nothing.

Worry was starting to prick at the back of my neck.

"Anything for you, guys? I've only found one reference. Fifty years ago, the symbol was found on a piece of paper that had been discarded in a rubbish bin in Sussex."

"I've got something, but it's not great." Neve pushed her book to the middle of the table and pointed to the drawing in the center. "It says that it's a symbol of dark death magic. Exceedingly rare. There's only one place in the library that might have that information. The basement."

"That's good, right?"

"I'm not allowed down there," Neve said. "It's got incredibly dangerous books, and only our highest-level staff have access."

Shit.

Neve frowned, chewing her lip. "It's important, isn't it?"

"Kind of a matter of life and death." Carrow hiked a thumb at me. "Her life and death."

Neve nodded, face pale, then leaned forward and whispered. "Let's do it, then."

"No. You can't." I gripped her forearm. "I don't want you getting in trouble."

"I don't want you getting dead, so I'd say I win."

"The stakes are higher for you, mate," Carrow said. "And anyway, Neve only gets fired if we get caught."

"Exactly." Neve nodded. "And I'm pretty clever. We can do this."

"What're we up against?" I asked.

"Guards and magical enchantments."

"We're going to need a distraction then," Carrow said.

Did someone say distraction? Ralph's voice sounded in my head, and I looked down, gasping.

"Ralph! I don't know if you can be in here."

Neve looked under the table and laughed. "Hey, buddy."

Hey, good looking.

"Ralph, be polite."

Neve reappeared. "Can you hear him?"

"Yes. He's my familiar. He said, 'Hello, Ma'am.'"

No, I said 'Hey, good looking'. And you can ask her if she has any of that American chocolate. Not the waxy kind—the good kind.

I nudged him with my foot. "Dream on."

"He could be our distraction," Neve whispered. "But he should hide under the table."

"No raccoons in the library then, huh?" I asked as Ralph scurried behind my legs.

"No. Which makes him perfect. Let's go." Neve stood, piling the books neatly on the end of the table and nodding to one of the imps.

The four of us hurried from the main part of the library, Ralph hiding between us and the wall, trying to maintain a low profile.

We made it to a quieter hallway when Neve stopped.

"We're going to head down the stairs, where we'll need Ralph to distract the guards."

I knelt down to Ralph's level and pulled my potion bag from the ether. Quickly, I fished around and pulled out a potion bomb.

Ralph made grabby hands, his eyes wide. *Gimme.*

"There's probably a reason no one ever lets you get your hands on potion bombs, so you're going to have to be careful."

Throw it and run, I'm no dummy.

"That's basically it, yeah." I retrieved a tiny vial from my cuff bracelet. It had taken a long time to make. "And this is an invisibility potion. Take it as soon as you've led them far enough away. I want you to get out of here safely."

"Would it be better if one of us took it and snuck in?" Carrow asked.

"Do you have only one?" Neve asked.

"Yeah, just one. They're rare."

"Then no. We're probably going to need all our talents for this break-in."

I handed it to Ralph. "You know the drill."

Payment?

"Of course. We'll discuss it when we get back to Guild City."

He gave me a skeptical look, then nodded.

I rose, and the four of us made our way toward the stairs at the end of the hall. Neve led us deep into the basement, past the attractive public floors, to the admin floors and, finally, to the dark, ancient halls of the oldest part of the building.

We reached a wide landing in the middle of the stairs.

"Almost there," Neve said.

A narrow door punctuated the wall to my left, and Neve pulled it open to reveal a closet full of old brooms. "We'll hide here while Ralph leads them out."

Ralph saluted, then ran off down the rest of the stairs, awkwardly clutching his potions. Worry shot through me as I watched him go.

"Come on." Neve pulled Carrow and me into the closet.

We shut the door and waited.

A blast sounded a moment later, followed by a shout.

Throw another. I need a distraction. Ralph's voice sounded in my head, as if he were shouting.

I yanked a potion bomb from my wrist cuff, then cracked the door and hurled it up the stairs. A massive boom sounded, and the stone stairs chipped.

Next to me, Neve winced.

"Sorry," I whispered.

Incoming!

I ducked back into the closet, hearing the scamper of little claws racing up the stairs, followed by pounding footsteps. A few seconds later, I peeked out, spotting Ralph leading two guards on a chase.

"Two of them," I whispered.

"Then we should be good." Neve ducked out of the closet and raced down to the next level.

We followed, spotting the area where Ralph had thrown his bomb. The old stone wall was chipped and blackened. Beyond it, a massive bronze door sat at the end of the hall.

We raced up to the ornate door.

"I've never seen it before." Neve craned her neck to look at the top. "It's...shit, it's big."

I reached for the door handle, and Neve grabbed my arm. "No!"

Too late.

As soon as I gripped the handle, my hand froze to the surface. I yanked but couldn't let go.

"Sorry," Neve said. "Should have warned you."

"You tried to stop me."

"It's okay. The door will release you when we get it open."

"How do we open it?" I asked. "Because it's definitely locked."

"There's a key somewhere, of course. But in case that is ever lost, the Order makes sure there is a second way to open their doors." She hovered her hands over the ornate designs on the door, clearly searching for something. "I bet there's a clue hidden in these designs."

"Let me try." Carrow pressed her hand to the door, her magic flaring slightly. Her gift included the ability to touch objects and read information from them, and she'd gotten really good with it.

I held my breath, heart pounding, as I kept trying to pull my hand from the door. I knew it wouldn't work, but I couldn't stop trying. Hopefully, she wouldn't get stuck as well.

Finally, Carrow opened her eyes. "So, I think we need to match the faces with the dates of their death."

I searched the door, finally spotting the faces hidden within the ornate, leafy vines but unable to see dates amongst the designs.

"There." Neve pointed to one.

I saw it. 1790, nestled right in a vine. We'd never have found it if Carrow hadn't told us to look. It was expertly hidden amongst the leaves. "How do we connect it to the proper face? And which one *is* the proper face?"

Neve pulled at the little curl of metal vine that wrapped around the number. It came away, and she could move it. "I think you're right, Carrow. But how do we identify the faces? The artwork is really rough."

She was right. I couldn't identify a single one as a famous supernatural or human.

"Let me try." Carrow pressed her hand to one of the faces and used her power. "Right. This is apparently Benjamin Franklin."

"No way." I tilted my head unable to see the likeness. "Really?"

"It's probably rough to make the puzzle harder to break," Neve said.

"Well, it's working," Carrow said.

"His death was 1790 according to my phone, which matches with this date." She dragged the vine over to Benjamin's face, where the tendril curled around it. "But I think that worked!"

"Let's keep going." Carrow pressed her hand to another face. "This is Napoleon."

"Still don't see it." Without Carrow's gift, we'd never have identified these. One handed, I typed Napoleon into my phone. "He died in 1821."

Neve found the date and removed the thin metal vine that curled around it, dragging it over to Napoleon's face.

Dark smoke was beginning to emit from the door, however, a noxious mixture that burned my nose. "Hurry, it's got a failsafe for if you're too slow."

"Shit." Neve searched, finally finding the face.

Together, we matched up the vines while Carrow Googled various dates. We worked frantically, moving as quickly as we could while the dark smoke seeped from the door. With every breath, my throat burned more.

Finally, we finished. My hand unstuck, and I pulled on the door. It was massively heavy, and I had to put my back into it, but I managed to get it open.

Neve slipped in first, and we followed.

Immediately, the room filled with thick black smoke —the same as before, but in such quantities that I couldn't see.

"Hold your breath and move," Neve said. "Another failsafe. An order member with permission to be here would have the spell to neutralize it, but I'll do what I can about it."

A faint wind began to blow against my face, carrying the smoke back toward the door. Neve was sculpting the wind with hand motions, funneling the smoke out into the stairwell. She made a gentle eddy so that it didn't rise up the stairs and give us away.

I followed her voice, stumbling through the dark as I held my breath. Soon, my lungs were burning and my legs weak.

"It's too far," Carrow gasped.

Shit, she was right. I had no idea how far the end was, but I was already in bad shape. I could breathe, but just barely, and every inhale was agony.

"We're almost there," Neve said.

Finally, the air cleared out entirely, and I sucked in a deep lungful of air.

"Thank fates." I blinked, clearing my vision. We'd passed through a dimly lit tunnel and now stood at the entrance to a small, dark library.

"Hell, it's haunted," Carrow said.

"No kidding." The entire space was shrouded in gray

light, the ancient bookshelves full of leatherbound volumes that looked like they only contained evil curses. Candles sat in chandeliers, and the old wooden tables were battered and worn.

I stepped forward, determined to get this over with. As soon as my foot crossed the threshold, a dark vine shot out from the wall and wrapped around my leg.

"Damn it." Neve grabbed me and tried to pull me back, but another vine shot out and wrapped around her arm. "The Order is so paranoid."

"What can I do?" Carrow stayed farther back.

"Don't come closer," Neve said.

Two vines shot out and wrapped around my arms.

Shit.

Quickly, while I still had a little bit of movement left, I pulled my bag from the ether and tossed it to Carrow.

She caught it just as the vines pulled my arms tight. More wrapped around my waist, binding me to Neve. We were squished together like peanut butter and jelly.

"There should be some acid bombs in there," I told Carrow. "Green glass. Round like a Christmas tree ornament."

"Acid bombs?" Neve's eyes widened.

"On it." Carrow fished around in the bag. "Found three."

"Okay. Be quick and pour them on the vines."

"Sure thing." I could hear her unscrewing the metal cap.

I craned my neck to see her dart forward and splash the acid on the vines near the wall. They withered, and two fell away from my right arm.

She kept working, quickly destroying the vines.

"Will there be an alarm of some kind?" I asked Neve.

"Maybe. We'll hear it if there is. But the Order also likes to trap people and leave them to rot. Rule breakers only, of course."

"Dark." I grimaced.

"Yeah, but good for us, in this case."

Finally, we were free. The library beckoned.

"Can I enter, or will I be jumping the gun again?" I asked.

"I don't know. I'll go first." Neve stepped forward, and nothing happened. "It's clear, thank fates."

Carrow and I followed, walking down the center aisle. The shelves stretched out on either side of us, disappearing into the dark.

"We need some light," Neve said. "Let's bring this place to life." She picked up a match and lit one of the candles. All the rest flared to life, but the library somehow looked even less inviting.

I inspected the labels at the tops of the aisles, searching for an organizational system. Yet it was all totally indecipherable.

Neve, however, began hurrying down aisles, pulling books off shelves and checking the covers.

"You can navigate this place?" Carrow asked.

"If there's one thing I'm good at, it's books," she said.

Thank fates.

We followed her, stopping in the middle of an aisle, and studying the shelf with her.

"It's one of these, I think," she said.

As she reached for one, a ghostly face appeared, emerging from the books.

I jumped.

The figure wore a white lace collar and tiny glass spectacles, looking like he'd stepped out of the past. With his bald head, he was vaguely familiar. I just couldn't place him.

"May I help you?" he asked.

Neve grinned sunnily and waved her Order badge at him. "Just doing a little research."

Did she know him? I didn't want to ask, for fear of alerting him to the fact that we shouldn't be here.

"Hmm." Skepticism sounded in his voice, but he said nothing. He also didn't emerge from the bookshelf. Just stared at us like a total creeper, face only half sticking out.

Neve withdrew a book, and we left the ghost, returning to a table in the main aisle of the library. He followed, drifting along with a suspicious look on his face.

At the table, Neve didn't sit. She put the book on the table and tapped the four corners, then the center, moving in a specific pattern.

I shot her a curious look, but she just shook her head slightly. Whatever she was doing—unlocking the book, perhaps—was Order business that I should probably pretend to know about. If this ghost suddenly decided we were intruders, we'd be in a hell of a lot of trouble.

The book popped open, and Neve flipped through the pages, finally finding the symbols drawn on one of them.

She leaned over it, reading quickly. I joined her, peering around her shoulder. As I read the words, dread uncurled inside me.

"Well, shit."

9

Eve

I stared at the pages, reading the horrifying details of the spell that had been placed on Garreth's grave.

The ghost drifted around to the other side of the table and leaned close. "Are you sure you're supposed to be down here?"

Neve's gaze snapped up to him. "Of course we are."

He frowned. "What about them? Where are their badges?"

"They're from another department, so they had to leave their badges at circulation. It's a new policy. More paperwork. You know how it is."

The ghost's eyes narrowed, seemingly unconvinced.

"Yes. In this world, nothing is certain except death and taxes. And paperwork."

While Neve tried to hold off the suspicious ghost, I flipped the pages of the book, looking for any more clues. There weren't any, so I straightened. "We're good here."

"Excellent!" Neve picked up the book and hurried back to the shelf, replacing it.

"Why are you in such a hurry?" The ghost asked. "No one hurries here. And three people coming to look at one little book?"

"That's not weird," Neve said.

"You're not supposed to be here." The ghost sounded triumphant, as if he'd just made a revelation.

He began to shriek, ear piercing screams that sent a shudder down my spine.

There was the alarm. Not traditional, and probably not all that reliable, but effective.

Neve raced out of the aisle, her eyes wide. "Shut up, Benjamin!"

My gaze flicked to the round glasses, bald head, and white collar. Benjamin Franklin? I hadn't recognized him before, but were we being ratted out by a founding father?

No way.

"Come on." Neve grabbed my hand. "They might not hear him, but there's a good chance the other ghosts will. It'll be like ghost phone tag, with us ending up on the bad end of an Order inquiry review."

We raced from the library, Ben Franklin shrieking his head off behind us.

As we left, I turned back and hissed, "Decorum, Ben! I'd expected more from you."

He glared and shouted louder.

Who'd have thought Ben Franklin would be such a bastard?

We raced down the tunnel. It went dark suddenly, and I looked back. The candles in the room had doused themselves. Blindly, I followed Neve, finally popping out in the stairwell.

We pushed the heavy door shut and took the stairs two at a time, racing toward the top. Every few flights, we stopped to listen, but no one was coming. At the top level, we slowed, straightening our shirts.

"Act calm," Neve said, then pushed open the door.

We stepped out into an empty hall.

Empty.

The relief was enormous.

"Come this way." Neve turned left. "We don't want to head straight to the exit."

We strode through the hall, and I tried to paint a bored expression on my face. I felt like a baby turtle making its dash to the sea, hoping a predator didn't appear and scoop me up before I reached the waves.

A ghost appeared to my left, rushing down the hall so fast that I almost missed her.

"She hears Ben," Neve said. "Soon, there will be a commotion. But we're almost good."

We made our way through the labyrinthine halls of the Order, finally reaching a side exit. She stepped out into the still-dark morning with us. The fresh air was a welcome relief.

"Let's get a little farther from the building," Neve said.

We followed her toward a large park that overlooked the lake beyond.

"Thank you so much," I said when we reached it. "Your help was invaluable."

"Will you get in trouble?" Carrow asked.

"Probably not. I covered my name when I showed Ben my badge, and he doesn't know who I am."

"Are there a lot of pretty red-haired girls working at the library?" I asked, worry working its way along my spine.

Neve shrugged. "Let's just say I'm good at getting out of trouble. It happens. A lot.

Good luck with everything." She gripped my arm and shot me a confident smile. "And be careful, all right? That was some dangerous stuff we found."

I nodded. "Will do. And thanks again. If you ever need anything, you know where to find me."

"Thanks."

The wind blew my hair across my face, and I reached up to brush it off my forehead. Neve's eyes widened, and she grabbed my hand, turning it palm up to reveal the glowing crescent moon. "This is cool."

I looked down at it. "Maybe. It's definitely new, and I have no idea what it is."

"A mark of power of some kind. I have one, too." She raised her arm. Peeking out from her leather cuff was a glowing design. "Mine has been growing though."

"Do you know why?"

"Not really." She grimaced. "That bit, I don't like."

"Well, if I figure anything helpful out about mine, I'll let you know."

"Likewise."

We said our goodbyes and used a transport charm to return home. As the ether sucked me in, relief surged through me. As least we were headed back.

Lachlan

"They're back."

I looked up at Kenneth, my second. He stood in the doorway, face flushed, no doubt from running here.

"Thank you, Kenneth." I rose. I'd spent most of the

last few hours staring at Garreth, which wasn't healthy. I knew it wouldn't give me answers, but I still couldn't help it.

The witches had responded a few minutes ago with the result of their test, and the information confused the hell out of me. But perhaps Eve had learned something in Magic Side that would lend clarity.

Quickly, I strode from the room, making my way through the tower toward the courtyard. I could feel the eyes of my people on me as I walked.

They wondered about Garreth.

We were keeping a murderer locked up in our dungeons. A cursed murderer.

The usual response to that was easy.

He had to be put down.

But I couldn't. Not yet.

Fortunately, my people trusted me. How long that would last, though, if they thought I was doing nothing...

I shook the thought away and headed out into the midday sun. The light was weak and watery as it filtered through the grey clouds. Without good weather, the courtyard was empty, which worked well for me right now.

Town was fairly empty, too, people having retreated inside for the workday. As I walked, I scanned every alley and rooftop I could see, looking for Eve's attacker.

He wouldn't have given up yet. As I approached the

alley that led to the Shadow Guild's secluded courtyard, I almost missed it—the smallest flash of movement on the rooftops above.

I squinted, moving left to get a better angle.

Yes, there was someone there.

They were moving toward the Shadow Guild courtyard. People in Guild City didn't make a habit of walking on rooftops, and the proximity to the Shadow Guild courtyard was too much.

It was the attacker. It had to be.

He was waiting for her to come out of the protection of her tower.

My wolf growled, pushing to break free. I forced it back. Though I empathized with my beast's anxiety, he was shite at climbing walls. I'd need to stay human to do that.

The attacker couldn't enter the courtyard because of the protections in place, so he'd no doubt wait on the rooftops. This was my best chance.

I reached the building and began to climb, using the windowsills as holds. Quickly, I scaled the wall to the roof, climbing silently onto the shingles.

The old buildings had peaked roofs, and I couldn't see him from my position. I scented the air, catching wind of him.

Still here.

I followed the scent, moving silently along the roof.

If I could just catch him, we'd solve a lot of our problems.

Silently, I climbed over the gables of an attic flat that overlooked the alley, approaching without a sound. The man crouched at the edge of the roof, perfectly still as he stared down into the Shadow Guild courtyard.

His clothes were dark and simple, sturdy jeans and a hooded jacket pulled up over his head. A faint wind blew toward me, bringing more of his scent—rot and mildew.

Dark magic signature. No surprise.

As I neared, my wolf fought within me, wanting to rise to the surface. To take over and sink its fangs into the man who threatened Eve.

Soon.

He was a big bastard. Bigger than me, which was rare. I'd be stronger in wolf form.

Finally, we were close enough. I called upon the wolf, feeling it rise inside me. It growled with delight, and magic swept through me, tearing my bones and muscles. The pain was brief, well tolerated after so long, and in moments, I'd shifted.

The world looked different this way, everything more detailed, my senses heightened.

The man stiffened and turned. Magic shadowed his face, making him impossible to recognize.

I lunged, reveling in the power singing through my muscles as I collided with him.

He grunted and tried to punch me in the gut. I moved, avoiding the worst of the blow as I sank my fangs into his shoulder.

We grappled, my teeth tearing into his flesh as he tried to throw me off him. Finally, I felt the magic surge within him. He shifted, transforming into an auburn wolf the same size as I.

His coat was covered in scars, and his eyes gleamed with a malice that was purely human as he snarled at me and lowered his head.

I prowled closer, a growl rising in my throat as the battle heated my blood.

His jaws snapped at me, and I lunged aside, avoiding the attack before launching one of my own, aiming for his shoulder.

My teeth sank into his muscles. Blood exploded in my mouth, an adrenaline surged through me, making my wolf go wild.

We rolled across the roof, the fight vicious. He was a strong bastard, and it took everything I had to keep him away from my neck. I wanted to keep him alive for questioning, but that might prove impossible to do and survive.

Our bodies were locked in a deadly tangle as we reached the edge of the roof and tumbled over. We fell ten feet, slamming onto a tiny metal balcony that had been bolted onto the wall high above the alley street below.

We thrashed, knocking large flowerpots off the ledge as we tore at each other's flesh with our fangs.

10

Eve

A crash sounded from outside, and I looked at Carrow. "You hear that, or was it just me?"

She stood from her spot by the fire in our main room, and I joined her, hurrying to the door and pulling it open.

At first, I saw nothing. The courtyard was empty. But movement from high in the alley caught my eye. The buildings were three stories tall, and a tiny Juliet balcony protruded from one of the upper flats that had long been abandoned.

Two wolves grappled on the narrow platform, a space far too small for their muscular bodies. The fight was vicious, and they seemed oblivious to where they were. Horror flashed within me as they tumbled off the balcony and plummeted to the alley below, landing on pile of broken flowerpots.

A flash of black fur caught my eye. "One of them is Lachlan."

"That other one is strong." Carrow frowned. "No one is supposed to be as strong as Lachlan."

"My attacker almost was." I stepped out, and Carrow yanked me back inside. "No way you're going out there. The attacker could have brought back up."

"But Lachlan." I tugged against Carrow's arm, fear snaking through my veins like poison.

Carrow gripped me tight, and Mac joined her, holding my other arm.

I called upon my fae magic. I'd used potions to buy myself the gift of lightning, and I called it from the sky, sending a bolt into the ground right next to the two wolves, hoping to distract the red one long enough for Lachlan to get the upper hand.

They didn't so much as flinch. But damn it, I couldn't send a bolt directly into them. Lachlan might take the hit.

Panic seethed inside me. "I need my potion bombs, let go."

"They're as dangerous at the lightning," Carrow said. "Those wolves are so fast you could hit Lachlan if he moves at the wrong time."

"I can help." Seraphia stepped out into the court-yard, raising her hands. Vines grew up from the ground.

She could do it. Seraphia was freaking Persephone, for fates' sake. She could tear them apart with her vines.

But Lachlan.

She might be too slow.

Frustration and fear bubbled within me, rising like the bubbles in a witch's cauldron. I couldn't take it. I couldn't just stand there, even if my friend was super powerful.

Magic surged through me, my hand burning. Every inch of me vibrated, a totally foreign sensation.

What the hell was happening?

My palm burned hotter, and I raised it. The glowing orb in the center of my palm was brilliantly white, and energy arced down my arm. Somehow, it felt like I was drawing power from the world around me.

But how?

It filled me up, making my head spin and my hand burn.

I have to help him.

Break up the fight.

Desperation surged through me, fueled by the new power that sparked within my skin. I nearly went blind from the intensity.

With a rending screech, the balcony above the wolves tore away from the wall, crashing down on top of the red wolf. Lachlan lunged away, avoiding the worst of the blow, then dived back toward the red wolf, who was scrambling to get out from under the balcony.

Despite the hit, the beast was still fast. He leapt over Lachlan and charged down the alley. Lachlan spun and raced after him.

My heart leapt into my throat, and I pulled at Mac and Carrow. Their grip didn't budge. Seraphia raced after them, sprinting down the alley, her vines following behind her.

"Holy fates, what was that?" Carrow asked.

"Me." I stared at the remains of the broken balcony. "Somehow, that was me."

Mac picked up my palm and looked at it. "Stopped glowing."

"I feel normal again." But worried. I stared into the alley.

I shouldn't care that Lachlan might be in danger. Sure, he was my mate. And that meant I was drawn to him. But it didn't mean I cared for him. That had to come naturally. Even fate couldn't provide that shortcut.

After everything he'd done to me, I definitely shouldn't worry about him. Hell, it'd be more convenient if the red wolf got him.

The thought made me feel ugly inside. I didn't mean it, but even thinking it was too much.

A moment later, Seraphia and Lachlan appeared at the mouth of the alley. Lachlan was bruised and bloody, his flesh torn in places where the other wolf had bitten him.

He strode up to me, his brow creased, and his eyes shadowed with worry. When he stopped, he gripped my arms and pulled me toward him.

"Are you all right?" His voice was rough with worry.

"I'm fine. You were the one in the fight."

His eyes flashed green.

He's trying to get his wolf under control.

I pulled back. "I wasn't in that much danger."

"He was watching for you. Waiting. That's danger."

"But I'm fine." I looked him up and down. Tension tightened his entire body, and his green eyes flashed brilliantly.

He was feeling the mate bond even though I wore the necklace. The overpowering desire to protect a mate could drive a wolf wild.

He cleared his throat and stepped back, trying to get control of himself.

"I suppose you didn't catch the bastard?" Eve asked.

"No, he has a healthy supply of transport charms, and he can shift quickly."

Just our luck.

"He couldn't get into our courtyard, though." Grim satisfaction flashed on Carrow's face.

Lachlan turned back to the remains of the balcony. "How did that happen?"

I looked at my friends, who frowned.

Don't tell him.

I didn't know what the hell was happening to me, but I didn't want Lachlan to know about it.

"I did it," Seraphia said. "With my vines."

He turned to it again, head tilted. There were no vines wrapped around it.

"They wither when I'm done with them," she said. "Now let's go inside."

She turned and strode inside, as if the matter were done.

And it was.

Seraphia was a goddess. Of course she could tear a measly balcony off a wall if she wanted to.

"I have information from the witches." He stepped forward, wincing. "Have you learned what you sought?"

My gaze fell to his wounds. "You're not healing like normal."

"I'll be fine."

"You're not healing at all." The wounds still looked just as torn as they had when he'd first arrived, spilling dark blood. He didn't heal immediately, but in the past, I'd seen improvement in his wounds over the course of minutes. "Was there something in his bite?"

His jaw tightened. "There could have been."

"Let me heal you before we discuss what we learned."

He hesitated.

"Don't be an idiot. Come on. You don't know how bad that could get."

He nodded reluctantly, then followed me inside.

"We'll be back down in a minute," I said to my friends.

"Sure thing." Carrow took her chair by the fire, and the rest settled in.

Lachlan followed me up the stairs, and I could feel his gaze burning into my back. We reached my cluttered workroom, and I gestured to a stool near the middle table. "You can sit there."

He sat, and I got to work. He was particularly powerful, so it would take an especially powerful potion to mend him. I turned to him and looked critically at the bite, going through ingredients in my head.

"I need to determine what the poison is." I picked up a piece of paper towel and walked toward him. "May I press this to your wound? I'm hoping it will pick up some of the poison that was in his bite."

He nodded, and I stepped close enough to press the paper to the gash in his side. He drew in a breath between his teeth.

"Sorry," I said.

"It's all right."

It wasn't. We were too close together. *Way* too close. At this distance, I could smell his forest scent and see the brilliant flecks of green in his eyes. Worse, his lips were so close to mine.

Not that I wanted to kiss him.

Of course I did.

No matter how complicated my feelings were toward him, I *definitely* wanted to kiss him. Especially after our last kiss.

I felt his eyes tracing over my face, warming me.

"Eve." His voice was low. Rough.

My gaze flicked up to his, and my breath caught at the heat in his eyes.

It seemed we couldn't stand this close without the bond taking over.

No.

I pulled the paper towel away and stepped backward. The spell didn't break, but it weakened, the distance helping me get some of my sense back. "That should do it."

I turned from him and went back to the table, working quickly. Chop, measure, pour, stir. I mixed up the potion quickly, dipping the bloody cloth in it when I was done.

While it steeped, I collected a poison identification book.

"What are you doing?" he asked.

"This potion will react to the poison on the cloth and give a clue as to its type. I'm going to use this book to identify it."

"You're talented at this."

"I had to be." I'd needed a way to make my way in the world after I left the pack.

"You could have stayed, you know."

I turned to him in surprise. "In the pack?"

He nodded.

I shook my head. "I really couldn't have. You didn't want me then, and you don't want me now. And it's the same for me. I couldn't stay and be forced into some bond that was bad for both of us."

Should I mention what the seer had told me? Did he know what the bond was supposed to do to me?

It was hard to say.

Anyway, knowledge was power. At present, he wasn't pressuring me too hard. I'd save it for later in case I needed it.

Anyway, what if he was the reason for my death?

There were a lot of ways the prophecy could play out, and until I knew more, I'd be holding it close to my chest.

I turned back to the potion and took note of the slick green sheen to the top of the liquid. It sparkled with black highlights, and I began to flip through the book, looking to identify it.

Finally, I found it. "Lycanthrophos poison." I frowned. "It's something specific to werewolves. Have you ever heard of it?"

He shook his head. "The mystery deepens."

"The book doesn't seem to know much about it, but

there's a suggestion for neutralizing it." I memorized the list of ingredients and began to collect them from around my workshop, gathering them up. "We're in luck, though. Doesn't take long to brew the cure."

"I was wrong. You're not talented at this, you're exceptional, aren't you?"

I looked back at him, warmed but wary. "Quit with the compliments. I don't understand you."

He looked surprised. "I don't think I understand myself, sometimes." His gaze turned serious. "But I meant what I said."

I shook my head and got to work, trying my best to ignore him. Ten minutes later, I had a bubbling grey potion that looked disgusting. "You're not going to like this."

"I've had worse."

"I'm not sure about that." I put it in a cup and handed it over. "Bottoms up."

He took it and nodded, then tossed it back with a grimace. "No, you're right. I don't think I've had anything worse."

"Here." I handed him a peppermint solution, and he drank it.

"Better. Thank you."

I looked at his wounds, watching as the edges began to slowly knit back together. It would take a while, but it looked like it was going to work. The poison was gone, and his body could heal again.

"Thank you, Eve." His gaze met mine, and a frisson of energy passed between us.

We stood too close, I realized.

Suddenly, it felt like all the energy in the room pressed in on us. I swayed toward him, drawn by his forest scent and the heat of his skin.

Awareness lit me up, sparking across all my nerve endings.

His brow creased as he studied me. "What is it about you?"

"Nothing."

He cupped the back of my head. "It's not nothing."

"I don't know what it is."

A ragged breath escaped him, and he lowered his head to the crook of my neck, breathing me in. His voice was ragged when he spoke. "You will be the death of me."

Same.

He pressed his lips to my neck, his movements restrained, as if he wanted to hold himself back but couldn't.

I bit back a moan, leaning into him. The heat of his breath seared me. The smooth press of his lips made my heart pound.

More. I wanted more of this. More of him.

No matter how we fought, how much I sometimes disliked him—*this* was always there between us.

The connection. The desire.

I turned my head, my lips brushing his. A ragged noise escaped his throat, and he pulled me closer.

"Eve? How's it coming up there?" Carrow's voice drifted up the stairs.

Lachlan and I broke away, panting.

I stepped back several steps and straightened my clothes, avoiding his eyes as I leaned down the stairs and shouted, "Just checking the truth potion I started brewing for Garreth. We'll be right down."

"Cool!" she shouted up.

I hurried to the potion, not looking at Lachlan. I could feel his gaze on me, though.

I'd almost kissed him back there. He'd definitely kissed me.

"Thank you for making the potion for Garreth." His tone was slightly stiff, but genuine.

"Sure." He wasn't going to mention the kiss, it seemed. Thank fates.

I checked on the little cauldron that bubbled on a side table, satisfied that it was finished. Quickly, I bottled up three doses, then put two in my bag in the ether. The last, I stuck in my leather cuff. I turned back to Lachlan. "All right, I'm done."

"Let's go discuss what we've learned." He turned and left the room.

I followed, grateful when we reached the main room that my friends were there to break the tension.

Carrow, Beatrix, Seraphia, Mac, and Quinn sat in the

couches and chairs, though Cordelia and Ralph were nowhere to be seen.

I took a seat on the couch next to Seraphia, and Lachlan remained standing near the hearth.

"The witches confirmed that the body belongs to Garreth," Lachlan said.

My jaw dropped. "Not possible. Not if he's also the one in the grave."

"That's what they thought. What I thought, too. But apparently, they're both him."

"There's no secret twin situation happening?" Mac asked.

"No. Definitely not."

"You sure? Because that's the most likely thing here."

"I would know if I had a third brother." Lachlan's voice had an edge of steel.

Mac raised her hands. "All right, all right. So he's not a secret twin."

"It's some seriously dark magic is what it is," I said. "We researched the symbols from the grave at Neve's library. And though there are still some gaps in our knowledge, we did learn that it was an ancient spell devised by Scottish warlocks centuries ago. It said nothing about leaving another version of him behind in the grave, but it did say that the living Garreth is here to stay."

Lachlan's shoulders dropped the slightest bit, as if he were letting out a relieved breath. It was a nearly unnoticeable motion, but the relief in his eyes was clear.

He was glad his brother was back, crazy murderer or not. I couldn't blame him.

"So it's permanent and not a temporary reanimation spell."

I nodded. It hadn't been what we were expecting—largely because it shouldn't have been possible—but those damned warlocks had figured it out.

"How did they do it?" Lachlan asked.

It was the part I hadn't wanted to mention. But I swallowed hard and forged ahead. "It takes three human sacrifices to do a spell like that."

"Fates." Lachlan dragged a hand over his face. "That's terrible."

"Whoever is after you—us—has been planning this for a long time, given how long ago Garreth died. And they were willing to go to incredible lengths."

"Which means that Eve is incredibly valuable," Carrow said. "Good thing you went into hiding so long ago. They might have found you sooner."

Holy fates. I'd never considered that before. Whoever was after me—would they have tried to find me a decade ago if I hadn't hidden myself away?

Shit. Did this have anything to do with the prophecy about my death?

"This has just gotten a whole lot more complicated," I said.

Lachlan nodded. "Someone used this magic on my brother, resurrecting him for a purpose. But he went after me instead of you. Was he supposed to go after me, or did the Dark Moon curse get in the way, forcing my brother to attack those he was once loyal to?"

"That means we don't know if the mastermind even knows your brother had the curse," I said.

"Seems like too much coincidence for them not to know," Carrow said. "But now they're after you."

"We have a lot more questions we need to answer." I looked at Lachlan. "Can we talk to Garreth? I have more truth potion."

Lachlan nodded. "Yes. Let's go."

11

Eve

Garreth's prison cell had been improved since I'd seen it last, with comfortable furniture and a rug.

Lachlan and I stood on the outside of Garreth's cell, looking in. My friends had stayed back at our tower, since we didn't need too many people for this, and it would just make it more stressful for Garreth.

He still sat on the floor leaning against the stone wall and staring off into space with a blank expression. I glanced over at Lachlan. He appeared stoic, but his creased brows and the shadows in his eyes made it clear he didn't like seeing his brother like this.

I couldn't blame him. Even though Garreth had

done terrible things, he'd been under the influence of the curse while doing them.

"Ready?" I asked.

Lachlan nodded and opened the door, stepping inside. I followed, watching Garreth warily. Last time I'd seen him, he'd had me tied up as bait. He'd planned to kill his brother as soon as Lachlan arrived, and he'd tried his damnedest to see it through.

"Garreth," Lachlan said. "We're here to ask you some questions."

Garreth stared straight ahead, his eyes entirely black.

Lachlan gestured behind him, and the two guards stepped into the room. I turned away as they restrained Garreth, peeking over my shoulder in time to see Lachlan pour one of the truth serums down his throat. Garreth thrashed, trying to avoid it, and my heart twisted.

I did not have the stomach for this. Lachlan wasn't torturing him or anything—not in a terrible kind of way —but this was still against Garreth's will, a miserable situation at the heart of it.

Finally, Lachlan stepped back, and the guards retreated to the other side of the cell. Garreth glared at Lachlan, hatred in his eyes.

"Remember," I said. "You don't get a lot of questions. So make them good."

"Who did this to you, Garreth? Who created two of you after your death, and set you on this path?

"The Maker."

Damn it, that was vague.

"Name?" Lachlan asked.

Garreth shrugged, jaw tight.

Lachlan looked at me.

"He'd be forced to answer if he knew. He doesn't."

Lachlan nodded and turned back to Garreth. "Have you ever seen him?"

Garreth shook his head. "Keeps himself a secret."

Of course he did, the shady bastard.

Lachlan looked at me again. "How many questions do you think I have left?"

"One, maybe two. Garreth is strong, and his resistance is powerful."

"All right." He turned back to Garreth. "We need a clue about how to find him. Tell me everything you know about where he is."

Garreth's jaw tightened, and he seemed to be trying to hold onto the information. But confusion flickered in his eyes, which was weird.

"Tell me, Garreth."

He frowned again.

"I think he's having a hard time remembering," I whispered.

"A pub," Garreth finally spit out. "A pub with a cat. And a sign that had a thistle on it. Human London."

Human London?

That was unexpected.

I studied Garreth. He looked exhausted, his face slack and his eyes hazy despite the pure blackness of them.

"That's it," I said. "It's all he's going to give us, and we should take a break before giving him another potion. It's a strain on the mind and risky."

"Riskier given that he's under the curse, I imagine."

I nodded. "Yeah."

I left, giving Lachlan a moment with his brother. He followed me almost immediately, the guards filing out after us and locking the door.

"This way." Lachlan led the way up the stairs and toward his quarters.

I stepped inside after him, taking it in. I'd seen it only once before, but it was even more dreary than I remembered. His flat was sparsely decorated—downright barren.

Lachlan was definitely a man who didn't care for the luxuries of life—or didn't allow himself to.

He strode to the fireplace, which flared to life as he neared, and pulled his flask from his back pocket, taking a swig. While he stared into the flames, I sent my friends a text.

We need the name of a pub in human London that has a cat living on the premises and a thistle on the sign.

Finished, I tucked the phone in my pocket and waited, wanting to give him a moment.

He turned to me. "Did someone make him like this? Beyond just the resurrection spell."

"Curse him, you mean? So that they could use him for their purposes?"

He nodded.

"Maybe." I could see why he wanted it to be that way. It would absolve Garreth of a lot of the responsibility if he was just a weapon. "Or maybe he was already cursed. I guess it depends on whether the Big Bad is also after you, and that's why he chose Garreth. Or if Garreth went off the rails."

Lachlan dragged a hand through his hair and cursed. "What happened to my father was terrible, but it was simpler, at least."

"With Garreth, you might still have a chance, though."

Hope flared in his eyes, and I realized it was the softest thing I'd ever seen on his face. "Do you think so?"

"Maybe." But it was a long way off.

My phone buzzed in my pocket, and I pulled it out to look at it.

Several pubs with cats, but only one named The Bonnie Thistle.

I read the text out loud to Lachlan. "It looks like we might have the next clue. We can go check it out."

"I'll go. You stay here, where it's safe."

"No way in hell is that happening." The steel in my voice could have built the Titanic. "You can't control me, Lachlan, no matter how hard you want to try."

His gaze flashed, but finally, he nodded. "You'll stick close to me, then."

"Fine." I looked at the clock. It was eight p.m. "Let's go. We have time to make it before it closes."

He nodded, and we left his tower, cutting across town toward the portal that led to the Haunted Hound. I had the address from my phone, and it wasn't too far outside Covent Garden. There were small pockets of human London where supernaturals lived and worked in secret, and maybe this pub was in one of those.

Quinn was on duty as we passed through the Haunted Hound, and he gave me a wave. I returned it, then stepped out into the secret alley that connected the Haunted Hound with the human streets of Covent Garden. It was full of fake rubbish bins that humans just walked by, never knowing what was beyond.

We exited the alley into the quiet hustle and bustle of Covent Garden. The Bonnie Thistle was close enough to walk, so we set off across town, headed toward Clerkenwell.

Lachlan and I didn't speak as we made our way across town. When we arrived, I tucked myself into the shadows opposite the pub. We stood on the other side of the street, watching it for a moment.

"Looks normal," I said.

It was an older building with a wooden front painted glossy black—eighteenth century, perhaps. At least, the facade was. The interior could be older.

"Quiet though."

He was right. I couldn't see many people through the windows, and no one exited or entered even though it was a popular hour for pubs.

"Let's go." He cut across the street, and I followed.

The pub wasn't as quiet as it looked when we entered. There was a bit more hustle and bustle beneath the low ceiling.

There wasn't a single supernatural in there that I could identify. The humans sat at little round tables and played darts in the corners. Several of them crowded around the old wooden bar as the bartender filled pints of beer. It was a fairly big place, though, and I could spot some smaller rooms at the back. It was a rabbit warren of a place, the kind of pub that had been around for centuries, expanding into the buildings around.

But it was all just so quiet and *human.*

"Do you think this is even the right place?" I whispered.

"No idea. Let's get a drink."

We approached the bar, and Lachlan leaned against the gleaming wood, making eye contact with the bartender.

The man smiled and strolled over. "What'll it be?"

"A pint of ale," Lachlan said.

"Lager, please."

The man nodded and turned to fill our orders. I studied him so intently that I'd be surprised if my eyes didn't burn a hole in his back. When he turned to me, he looked vaguely uncomfortable, as if he'd felt the keenness of my inspection.

I looked away. I was making it weird.

Lachlan paid, and we left the bar, strolling around as if looking for the right place to sit. Instead, we looked for clues.

And found none.

Finally, we chose a table in the corner.

"It was too much to hope my attacker would just show up and let us catch him, but I've always been a dreamer." I sipped my beer.

A small laugh escaped Lachlan before he drank from his pint, his wary gaze on the room around us. "If it's not the people, it's the place."

"But it's so busy. A supernatural couldn't do secret dealings here with all these humans around. He'd have to organize his cursed murder ring while standing next to the dart board."

"True enough." His gaze flicked around.

A woman appeared, coming from one of the quiet rooms at the back. She dropped into the chair across from Lachlan and me, glaring at us as she slammed her pint onto the table.

She was pretty and only a few years older than me,

with red hair and bright blue eyes. Though her clothes were mundane—jeans and a jumper—her magic screamed *witch*.

The first supernatural we'd seen. She must have been in the loo when I'd searched the back.

"What are you doing in my place?" she demanded.

I frowned at her. "Your place?"

She nodded. "Mine."

"You own it?"

"No. Todd owns it. But it's my local, and that makes it mine. No other supernaturals welcome."

"Does Todd know what you are?" I asked.

She shook her head. "And I don't want him to."

"Why don't you live in Guild City?" I asked. Could she possibly have anything to do with my attacker? Was she a coordinator for him, perhaps?

"Don't want to. Don't like the guild system."

"Not everyone does," Lachlan said. "But why take such a liking to this place?"

"Everyone needs a place, and this one don't bother nobody."

Places rarely made it a point to bother people, but I didn't say it.

"We're just here for a drink," I said. "Passing through."

But she had to know more than she was saying. As secretly as I could, I slipped a truth potion from the cuff at my wrist.

"There's really no other supernaturals who come to this pub?" I asked. It was weird that she wouldn't at least hang out with others of her kind, even though she did live in human London.

"No. Just how I like it." She turned and pointed to a huge man by the door. "That's Boris. He'll escort you out when I'm ready for him to."

While her back was turned, I flipped the cap off the vial of truth potion and dumped it in her beer, yanking my hand back right before she turned.

I smiled at her, heart pounding.

Suspicion flickered in her gaze. "What do you want here?"

"Answers," I said. She hadn't drunk the potion yet. But I needed to keep her talking so she would drink it.

"Oh, yeah? To what?"

My mind raced. "We heard about a powerful witch who lives in these parts. You're her, aren't you?"

She shrugged, a pleased look on her face. "Might be. Why? What you looking for?"

"Um—"

She brightened. "Too embarrassed to say?"

"Yeah." And too slow witted, apparently. I was a good liar, but I had no idea what her specialty was. What kind of magic could we possibly need from her?

"We're here about a problem that we thought you could help us with," Lachlan said.

Thank you.

She nodded and pursed her lips. "Romance?"

Well, shit.

Suspicion flashed in her eyes when I didn't immediately say yes. I jumped to fix it. "Yes. Romance, exactly. It's embarrassing, though, so you know...."

"Yeah. Hard to talk about, I get it." She took a deep drink of her beer.

Come on, finish it.

I needed her to drink the entire potion, but she put the beer down after one big sip.

Too much to hope she'd chug it like a frat boy.

Eyes bright, she reached for our hands. "Give them over. I can fix you two right up."

We'd just encountered a witch relationship counselor. *Great.*

I looked at Lachlan, who hesitated.

Was this worth whatever information she might be able to give us about this place?

Yes.

I stuck my hand out.

She gripped it, then grabbed Lachlan's and pulled it close. Her eyes widened. "You're mates."

"Yep." I nodded.

"But you don't want to be mates."

"Also yep."

She frowned. "But this has been fated forever." She blinked, her eyes seeming to go hazy. "Your bond is ancient."

I frowned. "Ancient?"

"Yes. Far older than just you."

Uhh...

"That's not normal for shifters," Lachlan said. "We have no lore that speaks about bonds more ancient than the beings they belong to."

"Well, you two are different." She shook her head.

I yanked my hand away. "I need a drink."

I picked up my beer and chugged half of it, hoping to encourage her to drink hers fast too. It didn't hurt that I was freaking out, and downing a whole beer sounded like a swell idea right about now.

She picked up her beer and drank deeply, then reached out for our hands.

I eyed her glass.

Half down.

Okay, so we just had to make it through one more round. Maybe two.

Lachlan hesitated, and I kicked him under the table.

He reached out, and we waited.

Her brow furrowed. "What is at the heart of your problem?"

"We don't want each other," I said.

"Yes, you do." She looked at me like I was crazy. "You *really* do."

Okay, fine. She wasn't wrong about that. "The dumb part of me knows he's my mate, so fine. You're kind of right."

Lachlan arched a brow at me, and I smiled widely at him. It wasn't like I was going to admit to wanting to jump his bones in front of this witch. *Or* in front of him, most importantly.

"But my rational mind doesn't want him. He's been a bastard ever since we were teenagers and we first met."

His jaw tightened, and something unrecognizable flashed in his eyes.

The witch nodded, pursing her lips. "Yes, he really was a bastard." She tisked, looking at him sharply. "That was mean, what you said. So mean, especially to a girl of fifteen."

Lachlan sat silently, jaw tense.

"He had his reasons, though," she continued.

My eyebrows shot up. "Reasons? Good ones?"

I could feel Lachlan growing more uncomfortable as time passed. I knew we were here to quiz her about this pub and the greater mysteries that stalked our lives, but this was getting interesting.

"He certainly thought they were good ones," she said.

"So he wasn't just being a bastard?" I asked.

Lachlan removed his hand from hers and drank his beer to the bottom. "Can I get anyone another drink?" His gaze moved to the witch as he stood. "What are you having?"

"London Pride. Thanks." She picked up her glass and pounded back the rest.

Jackpot.

Right at the time when I wanted to quiz her more about Lachlan. But he was striding off, clearly done with the conversation.

She leaned closer. "Be careful of that one. Hidden depths."

"Hidden depths full of monsters."

"Exactly."

12

Eve

I shivered, staring at the witch sitting across from me.

Hidden depths full of monsters.

It described Lachlan well. But what were the monsters? The Dark Moon curse?

Yes. But maybe there was more?

No. I needed to drag my mind away from Lachlan. She'd taken the truth potion, and this was our moment. I needed to be subtle, though. If I was, she'd feel compelled to answer but, hopefully, not register it as too invasive.

"There's really no other supernaturals who come here?" I asked. "Not even a trace of them?"

She frowned, her gaze going fuzzy. "No, I've never

seen—" She shook her head and rubbed her temples. "Actually, maybe I have."

"Seen what?"

"Sometimes in the morning there's a residue of dark magic on the air."

"After the place has been empty?"

"Yes. I'd forgotten about it, though." Her eyes flashed to mine. "Why would I forget that?"

Because someone made you.

I shrugged. "Maybe it just didn't register."

"Yeah." She nodded, clearly trying to convince herself.

Lachlan returned with the drinks and set them down on the table. I gave him a quick look, hoping he could read in my eyes that I wanted to ask the questions.

"Do you often see the residue of dark magic in the morning? Maybe it was a one-off, and that's why you forgot it."

She tilted her head, brow furrowed, as she tried to think back to it. "Yes, now that I think of it. More lately. A few times a week, in fact."

Hmm. Someone was using the pub in the off hours, and they weren't fully scrubbing away what they'd done.

"Do you practice your magic here?" I gestured between the three of us. "This kind of thing? Or do you also make spells to fix relationships? Like ours," I added for good measure.

"No real spell work—no. Just a counselor using my

gifts to get a feel for people. And yeah, sometimes I work out of here."

Hmm. So the person probably wasn't after anything that she was making. I sincerely doubted my attacker had any kind of romantic relationship, much less a trouble-in-paradise one that he'd seek help for.

Her gaze flashed to mine, growing suspicious. "You're here for relationship help, yeah?"

"Yeah. Thanks for it, by the way." I stood. We'd gotten as much as we could. I looked at Lachlan. "Ready?"

He drank half his beer, then rose. "Aye."

The witch watched us leave, confusion on her face. Together, we walked out into the night.

"I hope you got everything we needed, because I missed half of that."

"Yeah." I hurried across the street. "We need to find a place to wait. I'll update you."

I looked around the quiet street. Where would be hidden enough for us to wait while the pub closed for the night? My gaze snagged on the darkened windows of a flat above a shop. It was a risk, but it had a great view of the pub. I pointed to the windows. "Let's go there."

He nodded, and we found the narrow door between the chip shop and a florist.

Lachlan twisted the handle, breaking the lock with ease, and we stepped into the narrow stairwell, climbing to the top. I reached the door that I thought corresponded to the windows I sought and pressed my ear to it. "I hear nothing."

"Let me try." Lachlan did the same. His hearing was likely better than mine, given that he was the alpha. Strongest in body, but also in senses. "Empty."

He twisted the doorknob, and we slipped inside the quiet flat. The air was stale and musty, the place entirely dark.

"Thank fates, it's abandoned." I strode to the window and looked out, watching the pub down below.

"Well?" Lachlan asked.

"There's a hidden passage in that pub. I'm sure of it."

"Hidden passage?"

"Yes. A door somewhere, I think. She said sometimes there's dark magic on the air when she comes in the mornings. And there's no reason our target would be breaking into the pub just to use the space. There was nothing special about it."

"This passage must lead somewhere."

"Yep. Because he's not going there for her. She's not doing any magic he would want."

"So you want to wait until the place empties out and search for your passageway."

"Exactly."

"Well done."

I nodded. "Thanks. I'm good at this when I need to be."

He walked up beside me and looked out the window.

It was a narrow pane of glass, and he stood close enough that his forest scent replaced the musty smell of the empty flat.

"It's going to be a while," he said.

I nodded. At least a couple hours. Maybe more.

I turned back to the room and strolled around. Now that my eyes had adjusted, I could see the furniture. An old couch and some armchairs. Empty TV table.

I headed toward the kitchen, finding a bland space that had been designed sometime in the eighties. Idly, I opened a cupboard.

It was packed full of pots and pans, so many that they tumbled out. A large one hit me on the head, and I cried out, pain bright and sharp. The cookware tumbled to the ground with a massive crash.

"Eve!" Lachlan rushed in, concern on his face.

I clutched my head, eyes smarting. It had hit me just right, and my stomach pitched from the pain.

"Are you all right?" I felt his hands on my shoulders, gently turning me.

I opened my eyes and looked up at him, hand still pressed to my head. "Fine. Shouldn't have been so nosy."

"Let me check." He carefully removed my hand and inspected the wound.

As the seconds passed, the worst of the pain faded. In its place, his scent crept into my consciousness, followed by an awareness of just how close I stood to him.

I tried for a joke. "I make it out okay against a werewolf attacker, and yet I'm defeated by a pot."

"It was a big pot." He tilted my chin up to force my eyes to meet his.

"What are you doing?"

"Is your vision clear?" His gaze searched mine. "Any fuzziness?"

"No." I could see how ridiculously handsome he was just perfectly. The brutal beauty of his features was nearly devastating up close, and I felt my breathing go shallow.

"You're sure that you're all right?" he asked, his hand on my shoulder, thumb stroking idly.

"Yeah."

His gaze dropped to my lips and darkened with heat. We were only inches apart, and it was impossible not to notice. That same insane tension tightened the air between us, and all I could think about was the press of his lips on mine.

It was stupid. It was dangerous.

But I didn't care.

Standing so close to him, breathing in his scent, and feeling the strength of his hands...I wanted it.

I leaned up and pressed my lips to his.

A low groan escaped his throat, and he pulled me closer to him, pressing me full length against the hardness of his chest.

His lips felt perfect against mine—smooth and full, so skillful that it made my head swim.

"Eve," he groaned, his lips tracing a line down my neck. "We shouldn't."

I tilted my head to give him better access as heat exploded inside of me. "You're right."

But instead of pulling away, I ran my hands down his arms and back, wanting to touch as much of him as possible. I couldn't get enough.

Some kind of insane demon overtook me, making me slip my hands beneath the front of his shirt so that I could run my fingertips over the ridges of his abdomen.

A low, animal noise escaped his throat as he gripped my hips and lifted me up onto the counter.

"Yes," I whispered, wrapping my legs around his hips and pulling him closer as I tugged his mouth down to mine.

I kissed him like it was the end of the world. Ravenous. He clutched me close to him, pressing my core against the hard length of him. The feel of it made heat shoot through me, and I moved, seeking the friction and rhythm that would send me over the edge.

More, more, more.

I couldn't get enough. It wound me so tight with pleasure that I thought I might die.

"Take what you want." He moved his lips to my neck and bit down, not quite gently.

Pleasure exploded inside me, making me shake against him as my vision turned to starlight.

When it was over, I pulled back, gasping.

My eyelids fluttered open, and I saw his face hovering over mine, lips swollen and eyes dark.

"Lachlan."

He drew in a shuddery breath, then untangled my legs from around his waist and stepped back. The fierce erection still pressed against the front of his pants, and it took all my self-control to keep my eyes off it.

"That was a bad idea."

Embarrassment flooded me, and I felt my cheeks burn.

"It was good," he said. "Too good. Too dangerous."

"Yeah." I closed my legs and jumped down off the counter, still not feeling any better about the situation.

Of course it had been good. There was nothing but fireworks between us.

But he was right. It *had* been a bad idea. And I'd lost my mind over him.

He, on the other hand, had managed to stay completely in control. His still-raging erection was proof of that.

I am an idiot.

I knew he was bad for me. I hardly even liked him.

Yet I'd thrown myself at him.

"I'm going to go keep watch." I walked past him

without making eye contact, wishing that the floor would open up and take me to hell.

I could feel his gaze as I walked toward the window, but he said nothing.

Thank fates for small mercies.

For the next hour, I stood at the window, watching. Lachlan stayed in the kitchen, no doubt watching from that window. The pub slowly emptied out, until finally, the owner walked out and locked up.

"That's it," I said. "Last person has left."

Lachlan appeared in the doorway to the living room. "Aye, let's go. We'll try to find an entrance through the back. Less eyes."

Together, we left the flat and climbed down the stairs to the street, crossing quickly. There were few cars at this hour and no one around when we ducked into the narrow street at the back of the building.

It was dark and smelly but easy to find the back door of the bar. It had been marked with a sign identical to the front.

"Almost like people come through the back, sometimes," I said.

"Maybe they have gambling back here." Lachlan reached for the door handle and twisted.

The lock broke, and we stepped into a dark hallway. I waited for one tense moment to see if an alarm would go off, then relaxed.

I looked at Lachlan. "Shall we split up and look for a

secret door?"

He nodded. "I'll take the front."

I stuck to the rooms at the back, small snugs with little tables and benches built into the walls. The smell of beer and crisps still lingered, but the place somehow managed to have the abandoned feel of a bar that had been shut down days ago.

We kept the lights off as we worked, but there was enough illumination from the streetlamps outside. It didn't take me long to clear the rooms at the back. They were small and simple. I joined Lachlan at the front, finding him inspecting the wall around the dartboard.

"No luck, yet?"

He shook his head. "It's well hidden, that's for sure."

I cursed and spun in a circle, inspecting the space. "Maybe it's much smaller than a door."

"I've checked the floor for a hatch," he said. "There was nothing."

"Maybe it's a hatch set into the wall. Or beneath one of the booths." I called my bag from the ether and reached inside, withdrawing the same spray bottle that I'd used earlier at Garreth's grave.

"What are you planning?" Lachlan asked.

"This is a potion that reveals when magic has been used somewhere."

"I've searched for magic signatures and haven't found any," he said.

"I did, too. No vibrations or scents or anything. But

this will look deeper and find something that has been hidden."

"Good plan."

Only the rarest magic didn't leave a trace, and it was difficult to come by. Whoever we were up against was well equipped.

I found the proper potion and decanted it into the spray bottle, then got to work, spraying it in all the hidden nooks and crannies in the wall. The potion was an expensive one, but this wasn't exactly the time to start pinching pennies.

Finally, I got a hit in the far back corner of the bar, behind a booth that wasn't nailed to the floor like the rest. The wall was covered in an atrocious floral wallpaper, and there was no hint of a secret door.

"Lachlan," I called softly.

He arrived a moment later. "The outline is glowing, but the wall looks undisturbed. An illusion?"

"That's what I think." I reached for the wall and felt around. It was smooth for the most part, until I felt a handle that was invisible to the eye. "I've found it."

I pulled, and the illusion of the wallpaper disappeared, revealing a wooden door. It looked ancient, the handle far newer than the door itself. "I think this door has been here centuries."

"And someone only recently started using it again, from the look of the handle they added."

"And concealed with magic." I frowned, searching

my memory. "Humans used to build secret doors like this in the sixteenth century. They called them priest holes. They were for the Catholic priests who were being persecuted." And the existence of this one proved that the interior of this pub was older than it looked. What else was it hiding?

"And our target has modified it."

I shoved the spray bottle in my bag and climbed in through the door, scrambling out into a dark, dank tunnel on the other side. The air was stale and quiet, and the space narrow. I crawled forward, keeping my head low.

I squinted into the distance, using my cell phone torch for light. "It slopes downward as far as I can see."

"There are hundreds of tunnels beneath London." Lachlan followed me inside. "It could go anywhere. Let me lead."

"Too late. It's too narrow for you to pass."

He made a dissatisfied noise in his throat, and I had a feeling it was the mate bond that made him want to go first. Silly men.

Hand over hand, I climbed through the tunnel, my knees aching. "This is for the birds."

"Or rats."

A grin tugged at my lips. Finally, about a hundred meters later, we reached an area where the tunnel widened into a hallway. I stood, brushing off my clothes, and used my torch to shine light on the area around us.

"It's fairly modern," I said, inspecting the brick wall covered in graffiti. "Who the hell comes down here?"

"Besides our attacker, maybe kids. There must be other entrances."

He had to be right. There could be any number of ins and outs. If we came across our attacker, we'd have to be quick. He'd know these tunnels well and be able to escape out an exit we didn't know existed.

"Let's keep going," Lachlan said. "Try to keep your torch dampened so we don't give off much light."

I tucked the bright light of my phone behind the fabric of my shirt. It gave off just enough of a glow that we could see, but there was no brilliant beam to alert anyone to our presence."

Silently, we walked side by side, making our way through the brick passageway to one that looked older. The farther we went, the older everything seemed to become. The graffiti disappeared, and there was the faintest hum of magic.

"I can't identify it," Lachlan said. "Doesn't smell familiar."

"Can you smell anyone else?"

"People have passed through here recently, but no one I know."

The sound of rushing water came from up ahead, and I hurried toward it. "Is one of London's underground rivers down here?"

"Could be," he said.

We came to an intersection in the passage. In front of us, a dirty river filled a perpendicular hallway, rushing to the left.

"We'll have to cross it if we want to keep going." Lachlan pointed to some ropes that had been affixed to the ceiling and floor. One was low enough that a person could walk on it, and the other one was stretched higher up, no doubt to provide a hand hold.

I grimaced. "No thanks. I'll fly."

Lachlan nodded, and climbed onto the flimsy rope ladder.

I called upon my wings, feeling them flare to life behind me. I couldn't help but sense Lachlan's gaze on me, but I ignored it and flew across the river, landing on the other side.

He joined me a moment later, and we kept going. The hallway split off into rooms on this side of the river, but they all looked long abandoned. Some contained the detritus of earlier life—old beds, linens, even a few toys.

"Who the hell could live down here?" My heart broke to see it. "This place is terrible."

Lachlan stepped into one of the rooms and inspected the objects inside. "It's been two hundred years, at least."

"Still terrible." I kept going, peeking into every room we passed.

Some of the rooms appeared to have been occupied

more recently, but it was impossible to say when. Farther down, I found a room full of potion-making supplies. Nothing incredibly mind blowing in terms of ingredients or tools, but the fact that it was here....

"This is such a strange place to work." I inspected the supplies. "Do you think it has to do with my attacker?"

"Could be, if he's running a larger operation than we thought."

Once I'd determined there was nothing to be learned, I moved on. Lachlan joined me.

We kept going, finally coming across a row of wooden doors set into a brick wall.

"We're in a newer part of the tunnels again," I whispered, stepping up to one of the doors. There were iron bars set into it at face level. "I think this might have been a prison."

The sign on the door confirmed it. *Clerkenwell House of Detention.*

I stared into the empty, cold cell. It looked ancient and awful. I couldn't imagine being down here for any length of time, locked away without any sight of the sun. Or moon.

Lachlan stepped up to the next door, stiffening. He spoke, his voice was low with warning. "Eve. Someone is in here."

13

Eve

Ice cascaded over my skin, and I looked at Lachlan, who still stared into the prison cell, his face white.

A person?

Holy fates, this place was terrible enough when I thought it had been abandoned two centuries ago.

Heart pounding, I crept up to peek inside the tiny window. Lachlan moved aside, and I spotted her.

A woman, not much older than me. She was asleep on the floor, her brown hair dirty and her skin streaked with dust. Her clothes looked modern, though in pretty rough shape.

"We have to help her." I reached for the door handle, pulling hard. It rattled, staying locked.

She launched upright, awake in a second.

When she turned toward us, her eyes were wide.

And black.

Entirely black.

"She's a shifter," Lachlan said.

"And cursed." Horror hollowed out my insides. "Someone has her locked up in here. In *that* state."

It wasn't that different from Garreth's circumstances, on the surface. But in that case, we knew why he was locked up and, also, that we were trying to help him.

This woman...

Who had put her here? Had they cursed her first?

She could have fallen prey to the curse on her own, but someone else could have manipulated her circumstances to make sure she succumbed.

I yanked harder on the door, and it shocked me, sending pain singing up my arm. I removed my hand and shook it, hissing. "The door repels anyone who tries to open it."

Lachlan reached for it, pulling hard.

He grunted, then pulled his hand away. "We need to find a key. Unless you have a potion?"

"Nothing that can fight that." We still needed answers about my attacker, but our priorities had just changed.

I had no idea what we'd do with a woman who'd been cursed—the worst-case scenario was a mercy killing, like Lachlan had done with his father—but we had to try to help her.

"We're coming back for you," I said.

She hissed at us, glaring. Her jet-black eyes gleamed in the light. *Creepy.*

"Let's find a guard and take his key," Lachlan said.

I liked that plan.

Before we left, we checked the rest of the cells. No other prisoners, thank fates.

We'd gone only about fifty yards from the cell when Lachlan stiffened.

"Do you hear that?" he murmured, gripping my hand.

I paused, listening, and finally caught it—footsteps.

Lachlan pulled me into the next empty room, and we ducked into the corner, hiding in the shadows. I turned off my torch, and the room fell entirely dark.

Tension tightened my nerve endings as I hid against the wall, pressed to Lachlan's side.

"I'll wait until he passes," Lachlan said. "Then ambush."

I nodded, calling my bag from the ether, and withdrawing a potion bomb.

The footsteps neared, and I held my breath.

Finally, the person passed. Lachlan leapt out, and I followed.

There were six of them.

Oh fates. Somehow, they'd synchronized their steps or something. But there were way too many, and they were way too big. Each was Lachlan's massive size, and all were dressed in simple, identical dark trousers and shirt.

I hurled my potion bomb at the one on the far right, just as Lachlan charged the one in the middle. Before he could reach him, a blinding light exploded in front of us, followed by a concussive blast that threw me back against the brick wall.

Pain flared in my head, and darkness took me.

Lachlan

I woke in the dark, head pounding. For a moment, I couldn't remember my own name.

I couldn't remember *anything.*

Fear chilled me, cold and hard. I sat bold upright, memories rushing back.

Eve. We were somewhere in underground London, searching for clues about her attacker and trying to free a captured woman.

Not anymore. At present, I was locked in a pitch-black cell.

"Eve?" I whispered, heart pounding.

Fear licked at my mind. Had they taken her? Hurt her?

A low groan sounded from the ground to my right, and hope flared. I patted the ground, searching for her. "Where are you?"

"Here." Her groggy voice gave me a better idea, and I found her a moment later, lying on her back.

"Are you all right?" Gently, I felt around her head, looking for wounds. "Bleeding anywhere?"

"Maybe my head, but I think I'm okay. Help me sit up."

I did, afraid she would break apart if I moved too quickly.

"I'm fine," she said. "Let me just take a potion."

I heard her fumble with the cuff at her wrist, then snap off a potion vial and drink it. She sighed. "That's better. What the hell happened?"

"I remember a light. Pain."

"An explosion," she said. "Some kind of stunner bomb."

"They were prepared."

"And now we're in a cell like that poor girl."

I patted my pockets for my phone, wanting the light. "My phone has been taken."

"Mine too." A rustling noise came from near her. "Let me get something that will help."

A moment later, she pulled a glowing potion bomb from her bag. "Lucky for us, they can't search the ether."

The orb glowed a faint golden green, giving just enough light that I could see the cell door and the four short walls. It was a tiny cell, barely big enough for me to lie down in, and the walls felt like they were closing in.

I jumped to my feet and went to the door.

There was no handle on the inside, unfortunately. I kicked it, putting all my strength into it.

The door didn't even budge.

"It's enchanted," I said. "No give at all."

Eve cursed and stood, coming to join me. She ran her hands all along the edges of the door, clearly looking for some weakness in the magic. When she finished, she sagged backward. "I don't have anything that can fight that kind of magic. It's too powerful."

"You have no memory of how we got in here?"

"No, do you?"

"Not a one. It could have been your attacker, but I was too unconscious to say."

She began to pace, brow creased. "They'll come for us. That might be our best shot at escape."

"What about your familiar?"

"I can try to call him, but I'm not sure what he can do."

"Bring help, maybe."

"Good point." She blanched. "I don't want them to risk it."

"Your guild?"

She nodded.

"They'd murder you if they knew you resisted help. And they can bring members of my pack as well."

"Good point. They'd definitely murder me." She sucked in a deep breath and closed her eyes.

After a while, she opened them.

"Did it work?" I asked.

"I don't know. I've never done that before, but Carrow does it with Cordelia all the time. Hopefully, he'll feel it." Her shoulders sagged, and suddenly, she looked exhausted.

"Come, sit." I sat on the ground opposite the door and leaned against the wall, gesturing for her to join me.

She did, sitting a couple feet away and tilting her head back against the wall. "What's our plan when they show up?"

I frowned. "What kind of potion bombs have you got in that bag of yours?"

"Stunners, acid bombs, sleeping potions, a few explosives. Those are the most relevant ones, at least."

"Sounds good. Let's try that."

She nodded and pulled the bag from the ether, fishing around until she found what she was looking for. She made a little pile next to her, then handed me some. I piled them next to me.

Then we waited. The seconds passed by, then minutes.

"How are you feeling about Garreth?" she asked.

"He's a little more lucid, occasionally. For short periods. It's....good."

"That's fantastic. What if you could get him back, maybe cure him?"

"It seems too much to hope."

"Yeah. But to have family would be amazing."

The wistfulness in her voice punched me in the gut. "I'm sorry you lost your mother so young."

"You didn't have it any easier."

"I suppose not. Makes me understand what it's like, though." What a terrible thing to have in common.

She just nodded, and silence filled the cell.

When the little raccoon arrived, there was no announcement. No tingle in the air or pop of noise. One moment the cell was empty, the next, he was there.

Whoa. Not the nicest accommodation.

"Thanks, Ralph," Eve said. "So insightful."

I call it like I see it. Ralph frowned. *You're locked up, aren't you?*

"You think this is my idea of a vacation destination? Do you think you can alert the others?"

He nodded. *How do they find you?*

Eve gave him directions through the pub, and he watched her keenly, memorizing the information. His gaze moved to me, and he frowned. *Serves you right, for locking Eve up.*

I frowned. It was a certain kind of karma, except for the fact that she was also in here.

"He doesn't understand you, Ralph. Don't bother."

Yes, he does.

Eve frowned. "Do you?"

I nodded.

"No one else does."

"I'm your mate. I can understand your familiar."

"Like Grey can understand Cordelia. Of course. I should have known. Well, in that case, I'm with Ralph. Serves you right."

"Probably does."

I'm leaving. I'll come back after I tell them and try to find the key to this place.

"Thank you. If you run into our cell phones, grab them."

Ralph nodded and disappeared.

I looked at Eve. She appeared exhausted, and guilt streaked through me. I'd been a bastard to her. I'd been trying to suppress the thoughts of it, knowing that I'd been doing it to keep everyone safe. But my methods hadn't been the best.

And then I'd all but torn her clothes off.

She sighed and closed her eyes.

The guilt continued to tug at me.

What if this was it?

What if we didn't get out of this one?

I couldn't imagine going down like this, not when so many things had tried to kill me in my life, and I'd survived. But it could happen.

"I apologize." The words popped out of me before I could stop them. I'd had reasons for holding onto them, but they didn't seem to matter as long as we sat in this cell.

Her eyes opened, and she looked at me. "What?"

"I apologize for my cruel words to you when we were children."

"You were basically an adult."

I nodded, the guilt twisting my heart a little tighter. She was right. I'd been eighteen to her fifteen.

"I didn't mean them," I said.

"Sure you did. I wasn't exactly a looker back then."

"You were lovely." And it was true. She hadn't been the same flawless beauty she was now, but she'd been lovely all the same. And a light in the darkness to me, even though I'd seen her so infrequently. "My father was already falling to the Dark Moon curse at that time. I suspected it but had no proof. So I was hyper aware that it could be coming for me as well."

"What does that have to do with anything? You were stressed, so it made you act like an asshole?"

"In part, yes. But more than that—when I saw you, I knew. I knew that you could be the one to make me feel too strongly. There was something about you." He dragged a hand over his face. "I couldn't afford to feel anything that could bring on the curse. I couldn't let you be mated to a ticking timebomb."

Her eyebrows rose. "You were trying to drive me away."

I nodded. "And it worked."

"Hmm." Her gaze searched mine, and I wondered if my words were having any effect on her. She raised her knees and wrapped her arms around them, staring at me skeptically. "I'm not sure what to say. You could have just told me."

"You're right. And you don't need to say anything."

"What about locking me in the tower?"

I frowned. That had been so recent, I still wasn't sure if it had been a good idea or not. I'd known I'd done it to keep her safe, however.

"I—"

"Oh, don't bother," she said. "I can tell you're not really sorry for that."

I shrugged. "I thought it would keep you safe. I find that to be worth the consequences."

"Of my annoyance?"

I nodded.

"You haven't seen how annoyed I can get. I'm capable of some serious property damage. I enjoy it, in fact."

I felt a grin tug at the corner of my mouth, coming from nowhere. "I can imagine."

She looked at the door. "And when we get out of here, I'm going to destroy this whole damned place."

14

Eve

I stared at the cell door, Lachlan's words ringing in my ears.

I'm sorry.

He'd apologized. Well, not for everything. But for one of the big things. And he'd explained.

I had no idea what to feel about it.

It had been a stupid reason. Selfish. But it had been a reason. More than just him being an arse, at least.

He was wrong about my reasons for running away, though. His cruel words had only been part of it. But his apology made it clear enough that he didn't know the prophecy about me. Surely, if he did, he would have mentioned it.

According to the seer, running had been one of the best ways to protect my life. In his mind, he'd been protecting himself from the Dark Moon curse. And he'd been protecting me from him.

But he'd made no mention of the mysterious fate that the seer had prophesied for me.

He really must not know about it.

I closed my eyes and let the exhaustion sweep over me.

"Rest," Lachlan said. "I'll keep an eye on the door. It could be a while. I should be able to hear them approach."

I did as he suggested, trying to find a tiny bit of peace away from this miserable situation. At one point, I vaguely realized that I'd keeled over and rested my head against Lachlan's shoulder. He'd wrapped an arm around me, making a comfortable little spot, and I drifted off.

I had no idea how long it had been when his whisper cut through the darkness.

"Eve. They're coming."

I popped upright, heart racing. I went from zero to sixty in a flash, grabbing one of the potion bombs at my side as I stood.

Lachlan joined me, and we waited, the air thick with tension. Finally, I could hear the footsteps. They were close.

A key scraped in the lock.

I raised my potion bomb.

"I'll throw first," I whispered.

The door swung open, and a man appeared. I hurled the potion bomb. It crashed against his chest, exploding in a blast of blue light. He stiffened, and the guy behind him yanked him up, using him as cover.

Lachlan's aim was too good, however. He hit the second man in the forehead. His eyes rolled back in his head as the stunner turned his brains to scrambled eggs, and they both collapsed backward.

Behind them, four figures crowded in the hallway.

Too many.

One of them hurled a potion bomb at us, and I ducked, covering my head. In the tiny cell, there was almost nowhere to hide. It nailed Lachlan in the shoulder, sending him slamming back against the wall. The stunner knocked him out cold, and he slumped to the ground.

I chucked another potion bomb, hitting the man who stood right in the door, but one of his companions charged around him, grabbing me by the arm and yanking me to him.

I kicked, nailing him in the shin. As he winced, I lunged toward the ground, trying to grab up one of the potion bombs. A second guard was too fast.

He yanked on my arm, snagging the other one so quickly that I barely had time to struggle. In seconds, my hands were bound in cuffs and they were dragging me from the cell.

I yanked on the cuffs, feeling my magic being bound. *Magicuffs.*

I wouldn't be able to use my fae powers. Not even my wings.

Heart pounding, I looked back at Lachlan, who lay slumped on the floor, eyes closed.

Shit.

Worry streaked through me.

Please let him be okay.

One of the guards dragged his fallen compatriots from the cell, and another slammed the door behind us, locking it tight. The guard who held the key was the largest by far. Over six and a half feet, by my guess. The other five weren't much smaller, though.

Where the hell were they finding this army of giants?

Who was finding them?

"Where are you taking me?" I demanded. "Who are you?"

Silence.

I wasn't even sure they could talk, given how stoic their expressions were. There was something lifeless about them, though they weren't zombies or anything of the sort. Just brainwashed, musclebound dolls.

Just like my original attacker.

Were they taking me to him?

Fear shivered down my spine as they dragged me through the darkened corridors. This part of the tunnels was lit by sconces mounted on the wall and glowing with magical light.

I memorized the halls as we passed, determined to remember how to get back to Lachlan when this was all over. And I didn't let the key-holding guard out of my sight. That bastard was going down.

When they dragged me into a massive cavern, my jaw nearly dropped.

I'd never seen a place like this.

The ceiling soared fifty feet overhead. Maybe seventy. Really damned tall, at least. Massive pieces of ancient machinery filled the space, rusted and decrepit. There were dozens of pieces, some soaring thirty feet in the air, with pipes going all the way to the ceiling high above, ending near the grate that gave a view of the sky. Clouds covered the moon, which struggled to appear through the hazy veil.

It pulled at me faintly, like the feeling of having a friend nearby.

But what the hell were these massive machines?

Steam engines, maybe?

I wasn't a big history buff, but that's what they looked like to me. It would explain the grates leading to the surface above. They'd need a way to vent the steam.

Did my kidnappers have any use for these machines, or was it just coincidence?

My captors dragged me toward the side wall, where a man sat in a chair. When he rose, my heart dropped.

My attacker.

He was as massive and terrifying as ever—bigger than all the other men with a face so stone cold that he could have been dead. It was no longer shielded by magic, but it was so bland that I would have passed him on the street and never even seen him. He wore the same simple black clothing as all the other men, however, so if he was the leader, he didn't show it through his attire.

The memory of sinking my dagger into his back flashed through my mind.

Over and over, I'd plunged that dagger.

He shouldn't have been able to survive it.

And yet, he had.

There was something *so* not right about him. It vibrated in the air, making my hair stand on end and my stomach turn.

"Are you the one that Garreth said is after me?" I demanded.

He was definitely after me, but was he *the one*?

Was I dealing with The Maker, as Garreth had called him, or a minion?

The mastermind would have more life behind his eyes, right?

Maybe not.

"We all serve him." His voice sounded like it was

forced through gravel, and I got the impression that these guys didn't do a lot of chatting.

"Him? You mean Garreth?" Horror shot through me.

The blankness in his eyes calmed me a bit. No, Garreth was just a pawn. Like the woman in the cell was meant to be.

"Why aren't your eyes black?" I demanded.

They were wolves. I could feel it. And I'd seen the leader shift. Shouldn't they be cursed like Garreth if they were doing...whatever this was?

The man said nothing, just walked forward. "It is time."

His words sent a lightning bolt of fear down my spine.

"Time for what?" I struggled against the man holding me.

"Time for your transition," he said.

"Are you going to curse me?" I thrashed harder, pain biting into my arms where I tried to tear them away from my captors. "How do you give people the curse, anyway?"

He stopped in front of me, and panic made my breath grow short.

I had to get out of here.

Whatever he was going to do to me, I did *not* want.

A crash sounded from the far side of the room, and the man turned, searching the darkened space. More crashes followed, pieces of old iron machinery being pushed over.

Ralph.

He was creating a distraction.

Hope flared within me.

Above, the moon crept out from behind the clouds. When the brilliant white beams hit my face, power shot through me. Magic bubbled in my veins and strength filled my muscles.

The palm of my hand burned bright—pain and pleasure all at once. I was a live wire, filled with so much energy that the magicuffs felt like a flimsy plastic toy.

I had access to the sky, so I tried to call upon my lightning. It didn't work.

Of course it wouldn't.

Somewhere deep in my soul, I knew that my fae powers were still bound by the cuffs. But there was still so much power coursing through my veins that I could use. I felt like a soda can that had been shaken for an hour.

The leader stepped toward the commotion made by Ralph, gesturing for most of his guards to follow him. One stayed behind to hold me, and I watched them go, feeling the magic coursing through my veins, demanding to be let out.

It was breaking through the magicuffs.

It felt like the moon was feeding its power directly into me, like we were connected by a wire. It kept pouring its magic into me until I raised my hands, needing to let it out.

I chose my target—one of the massive pieces of steam machinery.

Just like the Juliet balcony, but bigger. My entire body vibrated as I yanked it from its spot and hurled it at the group of men who were walking toward Ralph, scattering them like bowling pins.

My jaw dropped.

Holy fates.

The guard behind me yanked hard. "Stop that."

"You're kidding, right?" I stomped on his foot and jerked myself away so hard that his grip broke.

"Hey!" He lunged for me, but I kicked out, nailing him right in the balls.

He grunted and slowed but didn't stop. I had long enough to dart away, however, and I used my strange new magic to slam another piece of machinery into him. He went down hard, lying silently beneath the crumpled metal.

I spun around, spotting several of the men climbing to their feet from beneath the massive pile of iron that I'd thrown at them. The power of the moon still coursed through me, and I threw another piece of machinery at them, smashing them to the ground once again.

Ralph charged out from behind the machinery that he'd been hiding behind. *There are more.*

"How many?" I demanded, searching for the guard

who had held the key to our cell. They were down for now, but not dead. Not all of them, at least.

Lots. I don't know. A dozen? Maybe more.

Too many to fight right now. We needed to get the hell out of here and get backup.

"Help me find the key."

He nodded and launched into the pile of twisted metal and bodies. I heard him digging around, and he popped out a moment later with a ring of keys in his little hand. *That guy is definitely dead.*

"Good riddance. What about the boss? The one who attacked me?"

Couldn't tell. He was strong though.

"Probably alive, with my luck." But too buried beneath the metal for me to find him quickly. I wasn't sure I could stomach trying to kill an unconscious man anyway, no matter how great a threat he was.

"Come on, get me out of these." I knelt and held out my hands so that he could unlock the cuffs.

He worked quickly, freeing me in seconds.

"Let's go get Lachlan out."

We raced away from the pile of bodies, sprinting down the darkened halls until we reached the cell. Ralph tossed me the key, then pulled a loose brick out of the wall and fished around inside.

"What are you doing?" I asked as I stuck the key in the lock.

He pulled out two cell phones. *I stole them back but needed somewhere to hide them.*

"Clever."

Very. And you owe me.

I turned the key and cracked open the door. "It's me."

"Thank fates." Lachlan pulled the door open from the inside. "Are you okay?"

His eyes were shadowed with worry, his jaw tight.

"Fine. Let's get out of here. There are too many to fight. We'll return with backup."

"All right."

We headed down the hall, stopping at the cell door of the woman we'd seen earlier. She was still there, eyes still black as pitch. I fumbled with the key ring, trying to find the proper key. One after the other, I tried them all.

"None are working!" Frustration cracked in my voice.

"I can't break the door down. We'll have to come back for her."

I hated to leave her, but he was right. It was the only way. If they caught us again, I couldn't guarantee that we'd get out.

"Let's go."

I gave her one last look. "I'm coming back, I promise."

She just stared, expression dead, and I hoped I wasn't already too late to save her.

Come on, I hear them.

Lachlan tugged on my arm, and I followed. Together, we raced from the cell, sprinting through the tunnels as we tried to retrace our steps back to the priest hole in the pub. Ralph followed us, tiny feet moving fast.

Minutes passed as we ran, every one of them feeling like an eternity. Finally, we reached the narrow tunnel that led up to the pub. Ralph raced ahead. I dived in and began to crawl, heart racing.

When I reached the door, I pushed it open, letting Ralph out first. Then I spilled out into a nearly empty pub, scrambling to give Lachlan room to get out, too. He followed, and we stood, dusting ourselves off as a woman turned to look at us, her eyes wide.

She was one of the staff, from the look of her uniform, and it was sometime in the morning. They probably hadn't officially opened, yet.

"What the bloody hell do you think you're doing?" she demanded.

I pulled a vial of forgetfulness powder from my wrist cuff and uncorked it, then blew it in her face.

She coughed, her eyes going wide, then stared at us dumbly.

"She won't remember anything from the last ten minutes or the next ten," I said.

"Good."

We left her there, departing the little room at the back and heading into the main part of the pub.

I nearly slammed into Carrow, grabbing her shoulders at the last minute so our heads didn't smash together. Beatrix, Mac, Seraphia, and Quinn were behind her. Six shifters had accompanied them—the best of Lachlan's security force, from the look of it.

"Eve!" Carrow hugged me close. "You made it out!"

"Yeah. Thank you for coming."

"We haven't been able to find the damned priest hole," she said. "Mac was able to fog the waitress's mind a bit, but she was starting to get suspicious."

I looked at Lachlan and Ralph. "Is this enough, do you think? Should we go back in?"

Ralph twisted his little hands, inspecting the crowd. *Maybe? I saw more than a dozen, but don't know how many were hidden.*

"We could try," Lachlan said.

"Are we going back to fight someone?" Carrow asked. "Because I could be into that."

"Yeah. There's someone we need to rescue. And now that we have backup, we should do it." I turned and hurried back to the priest hole, feeling for the handle.

But it was gone.

Shit.

No matter how I touched the wallpaper, looking for the hidden handle, it wasn't there.

I turned to look up at my friends, who were staring down at me. "It's gone."

"Gone?" Lachlan asked.

"Yeah. There must be some kind of remote magic,

and they blocked it." I called my bag from the ether and fished around until I found the spray bottle that I'd filled with the magic-revealing potion.

Quickly, I spritzed it on the wall. All it did was make it wet. I could feel the confused gaze of the waitress on us as I turned to look back at my friends. "Definitely gone."

"The tunnel could still be there, though," Lachlan said. "Behind the wall, right?"

"Maybe?" I looked at the waitress. "Do you have any tools in the back? A sledgehammer or anything?"

She grimaced, still slightly foggy from the potion I'd blown in her face, but not so foggy that she didn't know that was a weird request.

"I'll help her find it," Mac said.

"And we'll make sure no one else enters the bar," Quinn said.

A few minute later, Mac and the waitress returned with a crowbar and sledgehammer.

"There's a construction site down the road," she said.

"Thanks." I stood, reaching for the sledgehammer.

Lachlan got it first, however, and pulled the booth farther away from the wall so that he could work. He gave the confused waitress a quick look. "We'll pay for damages."

Then he slammed the heavy iron tool against the wall.

Ten minutes later, it was confirmed. The tunnel was gone.

Like, *gone* gone.

I slumped back against an old booth. "They filled it in."

"That quickly?" Mac asked. "It was seconds."

I shrugged. "Magic of some kind, though I don't know what."

"There has to be another way in," Lachlan said.

"Many, I would think. Those tunnels were huge. And ancient."

"We'll head back to Guild City and make a plan then." Lachlan turned to the shifters. "Will two of you stay and clean this up? Then make arrangements with the waitress so that we can cover the cost of repairs."

The man nodded. "Aye, boss."

"Thank you."

I looked at the chaos that was the wall, praying that we'd be able to find another way in.

15

Eve

We reached Guild City an hour later, returning to our tower for safety. I doubted my attacker would be stalking me through the streets at this exact moment, but who knew?

Especially since I'd probably almost killed him. With my luck, he'd recovered quickly from his run-in with a steam engine and was already on his way here.

The seven of us—Lachlan included—piled into the chairs and couches that filled the room. His four shifter guards waited outside by the door.

"I'll be back with snacks," Mac said. "You look like you could use a bite."

My stomach grumbled audibly at the word snacks, and I nodded my thanks.

"So?" Carrow asked.

"Where to begin?" I gave her the rundown, omitting the part about my new magic. I didn't want to say it in front of Lachlan just in case.

In case of what, I wasn't sure.

But even though he'd apologized for the past, we weren't on an even footing yet. My secrets would stay my secrets. Especially the ones I didn't understand.

"How did you get away from them?" Lachlan asked.

"Ralph. There was a collection of massive old steam machinery. He set off a chain reaction in there, making it collapse on our kidnappers."

Lachlan frowned, seeming to have a hard time buying it.

I'm very talented. Ralph gave a toothy grin.

Lachlan studied him. "All right."

I still had no idea if he believed me or not, but Carrow spoke up. "How are we going to find a way in?"

"I can search the library," Seraphia said. "Those tunnels beneath Clerkenwell are ancient. There would be record of them somewhere. The ins and outs must have been written down."

"The dwarves' guild might know as well," I said. "They know all about underground London."

"So our plan is to find another entrance, break in,

save the prisoner, and capture your attacker," Lachlan said. "What did he want with you?"

I hadn't mentioned that part either, and Lachlan was clearly suspicious. It made it worse that my friends hadn't questioned me harder, no doubt knowing that I was keeping some cards close to my chest.

But I had to tell the truth somewhere, and this was vague enough. "He said it was time for the transition."

"To death?" Lachlan asked.

"I'm not sure if that's what he wants." I frowned. "Wouldn't he have just killed me sooner if it was?"

"You're right," Carrow said. "He didn't use a weapon against you when he attacked you in the city. If he really wanted to kill you, he'd have hedged his bets and brought a weapon."

"So he wants me for something. And worse, I don't think he's the boss. He said *we all serve him.*"

"That's got serious minion vibes," Mac said.

"My brother might know more," Lachlan said. "If they've got another victim down there like him, he could know her. It's another avenue of questioning, at least."

It was a good point. Garreth seemed to do best when we gave him specific prompts. Otherwise, he was like a windup doll—just sitting there until someone put some effort into it.

I pulled my bag from the ether and found my last truth potion, handing it over to him. "You can go question him with this if you want."

He took the vial, his fingertips brushing mine. A spark raced up my arm, and I barely managed to hold his gaze without looking away like a ninny.

"You won't come?" he asked.

"I think we have too much to do and not enough time. I'm going to help look for another entrance."

He frowned.

"We need to split up," I repeated, voice hard.

"Fine. I'll send some guards with you."

"All right."

He nodded and stood, turning to my friends. "Thank you for coming for us."

"Duh." Carrow grinned. "But you're welcome."

He nodded, then left. On the doorstep, he leaned close to speak to his guards, shutting the door behind him as he spoke. I watched him, feeling my friends' gazes on me.

As soon as the door shut behind Lachlan, the four shifters stared at me.

Carrow said, "Well? Spill. Because something else clearly happened."

I raised my hand and showed them my palm. "Apparently I'm super telekinetic."

"What?" Her eyebrows shot up.

"Yeah. They put magicuffs on me, but as soon as I got a look at the moon, my magic went haywire. Even the cuffs couldn't hold me."

"Whoa." Mac sat back.

It was totally bad ass.

"They can't hear you, Ralph."

It was still bad ass.

"And scary," I said.

"Do you have any idea why?" Mac asked.

"Not a clue." I looked at my palm. "But I'm pretty sure this orb is the moon."

"And you're getting your power from the moon," Carrow said.

"Maybe? I felt it so strongly." I thought back to the attack in our courtyard when I'd yanked the Juliet balcony off the wall. "I couldn't see the moon when I took out the attacker in our courtyard, but it would have been there anyway."

"What kind of supernatural can harness the power of the moon?" Carrow asked.

"A fancy shifter?" Mac said.

"Our power doesn't really work that way," Quinn said. "Eve is something else."

"Maybe I got it from my father."

"Whatever it is, I think it might be the reason that bastard is after you."

It made the most sense. "Well, we'll stop him before he can get me."

"Damn straight." Carrow stood. "We need to start looking for ways into the Clerkenwell tunnels."

"I'll head to the library," Seraphia said.

"We can go see the dwarves." Carrow met my gaze. "Good with you?"

"Yeah. Let's go see what they know."

"We'll help Seraphia search." Mac gestured between her, Quinn, and Beatrix.

"Thanks, guys."

"'Course." Mac grinned.

We split up, heading out into Guild City. As Carrow and I walked, we stuck to the main streets, ever wary of our surroundings. The shifters stayed about fifteen feet behind us. Fortunately, the High Street was relatively crowded, full of people carrying shopping bags and chatting away as they walked from shop to shop.

"I seriously doubt they're stalking me right now," I said. "But I can't shake the feeling I'm being watched."

"Smart to be wary." Carrow looked up toward the roofs.

A few minutes later, we reached the dwarves' part of town. I rarely came this way since it was the posh part of the city. The buildings were slightly larger and the streets quieter, all well manicured with flowers in planters and window boxes. Instead of shops on the bottom floors, there were residences—the kind of places with gleaming black doors that screamed old money. Many of the Tudor facades had been replaced with plaster and brick, though they were still historic.

The dwarves' guild was one of the wealthiest in town. They made their money by mining gold found beneath London. According to human geologists, London wasn't gold territory. None of England was—not in the way of the Yukon or Sweden. That's just what the dwarves wanted them to think.

We reached the courtyard in front of their guild tower. It was a tidy garden of pebble pathways and flower beds leading up to a short, squat guild tower built of massive stones. The entire building vibrated with eerie quiet.

We stopped in front of the door, and Carrow leaned close. "You have a slightly new signature. It feels like moonlight. See if you can get that tamped down."

"Shit, really?"

"Yeah."

I drew in a steady breath and tried to wrangle the new magic, but it was difficult. I still barely had control of it—and I certainly had no idea what it was. But I didn't want to be flashing it around the dwarves or anyone unfamiliar until I knew what it was.

"That's better." Carrow knocked on the door, and we waited.

A few minutes later, it swung open to reveal a beautiful room with gleaming wood floors and rose wallpaper. A short, stout man stared up at us. His full beard was intricately braided, threaded through with gold and rubies. His scarlet suit was perfectly tailored, and the brilliant yellow tie should have looked terrible against it.

Instead, he looked dashing as hell.

The dwarves really were known for their fashion, and this one did not disappoint.

"Madams. I'm afraid to tell you that the dining room is not yet open."

"We're not here for The Cellar," I said. It was one of the most famous restaurants in town and definitely out of my budget.

"We'd like to see Ogden the Bold," Carrow said. "I'm Carrow Burton. He knows me."

"He knows many people. That doesn't mean he'll see you."

"Can you please just ask?"

He harrumphed, then turned, leaving us standing in the doorway. A few moments later, he returned. "You may follow me."

I was going to take that as a good sign.

Carrow and I followed him down a staircase and into a long, narrow room. Small tables marched down the space, each covered with ivory linen and brilliant floral arrays. Golden light gleamed from the arched brick ceiling, and I whistled low. "No wonder people pay so much to eat here."

"Only people with the finest taste," the dwarf said.

I grinned. He was *definitely* implying that wasn't me.

He wouldn't be wrong. I could appreciate this kind of thing, but it was far from my normal.

"You may sit there." He gestured to a large table.

We sat, putting our backs to the wall so that we could look down the long space.

"So, you and Lachlan," Carrow said.

"Yeah. That."

"Seems different."

"Maybe a little."

"But you're still opposed to the mate bond."

"Oh, definitely. He apologized for being a dick when we were kids, and he had his reasons, but..."

"Do you believe the reasons?"

"Yes." Definitely. Lachlan could be a bastard, but there was one thing about him that was indisputable: he was loyal to his pack. He'd do anything to fulfill his role as alpha, and the most important part of that was holding off the effects of the Dark Moon curse. If he really thought I could make him feel too strongly...

The idea made me shiver.

Could I really do that? Break through the cold that surrounded him?

No. 'Course not.

"He looks at you differently," Carrow said. "He always looked at you differently, but this is something else. Even more than before."

I rubbed my arms, having no idea how to interpret that. "He's a mystery to me."

A moment later, Ogden appeared. At least, I assumed it was Ogden. I'd never met the guy. His beard extended to the middle of his chest, so heavily studded with gems that he had to be the boss. He also wore an impeccably tailored suit—this time in Kelly green with a blue tie.

"Carrow Burton." He studied my friend, his brow creased. "I have to assume you have a problem if you are here at this hour."

"I do. Thank you for meeting with us, Ogden." Carrow gestured to me. "This is my friend Eve. We're looking for entrances to the tunnels beneath Clerkenwell."

He sat across from us. "Are you now?"

"Do you know of any?"

"I do, though many of them were blocked by an unknown person recently."

"How recently?"

"Within the last few weeks. We don't tend to go into Clerkenwell, but there were a few entrances into that area from our mining tunnels to the west. They're blocked, though."

I looked at Carrow. "They've been setting up their creepy headquarters for a while."

"Do you know who is doing it? And why?" Ogden leaned forward, his eyes gleaming with interest. "We don't like new people on our turf."

"I've met them, but I don't know who they are," I said. "I do know that they're bad news. One of them has been trying to kidnap me, and they have other prisoners down there. At least one woman." I didn't mention the curse. It was the shifters' business, and Ogden didn't need to know.

His brow furrowed and his gaze turned thunderous. "The Below shouldn't be used that way."

"My thoughts exactly."

Protectiveness edged his voice. "We'll help you. What do you need?"

Thank fates. "A map of the entrances would be great."

He nodded. "You'll have it. We can also check the ones that are underground to see if any of them have weak spots we can dig through."

"Do you know of any entrances on the surface?" Carrow asked.

He nodded. "A few. Likely not all."

"It'll help. Thank you."

Ogden nodded and stood. "I'll be right back."

We watched him go, and Carrow leaned close. "This has potential."

"Yeah, thank fates." I frowned. "I'm sick of waiting for him to ambush me. I'd rather take the fight to him."

"Exactly."

A few minutes later, Ogden returned. He clutched a rolled-up paper in his hand, along with a small metal tool. "I have two things for you."

He laid the map out on the table and set the strange metal device next to it. The brass object looked ancient —and almost like a compass. He pushed it toward me. "You don't have a dwarves' gift for navigating underground, but as you're determined to go down there, I think you'll find this handy. It is enchanted to lead you to the nearest exit."

"At the surface?" I picked it up and inspected the tiny spinning dial.

"Yes."

"This could be a life-saver," I said.

"Exactly. We don't need you dying in the Below. Like to keep it nice and tidy down there."

"You're a bleeding heart, Ogden," Carrow said.

He grumbled, then pointed to the map. "These are your above-ground entrances, these are the below."

I followed his finger as he moved it, taking in three above-ground entrances and four below. I pulled out my cell phone and snapped some pictures.

"You can take it with you," Ogden said.

"Thank you. I just want to send these to Lachlan. My guild doesn't have the manpower to check out the surface entrances to see if they're still open, but his does."

"Good thinking," Carrow said.

I sent off the texts, then looked back at the map. It was a labyrinthine collection of twisting underground passages, so many that it would take months to explore them all. Without the map, we'd be screwed.

"It's only part of the Below," Ogden said, pride in his voice. "There's a whole world down there."

"You truly are a lifesaver, Ogden."

He grumbled but sounded pleased.

I rolled up the map and stuck out my hand. "Thank you."

He shook my hand, then Carrow's. "I'll lead you out."

Together, we climbed the stairs back to the surface level and headed out into the city.

At the doorstep, he turned to us. "I'll let you know soon about the status of the underground entrances. If we can get in, we'll do it."

"Thank you."

We departed, heading back toward our tower. My shifter guards fell into step behind, giving us just enough room for privacy.

"I'll check with Seraphia," Mac said. "See what she found at the library."

As we walked, I kept a wary eye on the rooftops. My attacker seemed to prefer them, and the last thing I needed was to get dragged back there before we were ready to fight.

"She's still at the library," Mac said.

"Let's meet her there."

We stuck to the busiest streets in town as we made our way there. We reached Seraphia's library a few moments later and crossed the street toward the small Tudor building. It had the ramshackle look of some of the older buildings in town—the dark wooden beams were somewhat slanted, and the diamond pane windows completed the charming affect. We stepped through the small wooden door into the cavernous interior.

"I'll never get over this place," Carrow said.

Despite its tiny outside, it was roughly the size of Neve's library, with a massive domed roof overhead and expansive marble floors.

Seraphia hurried forward from the back, her hair piled in a messy knot on her head. Behind her, a massive man in a dark cloak sat at a table, his black hair falling over his brow as he looked through a book.

Hades.

I hadn't seen him in a while. Seraphia's mate spent most of his time in the Underworld, which was accessible through a portal in her library. He stood out like a sore thumb in Guild City in his black warrior's garb.

"He came to help look," Seraphia said.

"I came for lunch," he said, not looking up from his book.

"Well, this was what you got." Seraphia shot him a smile over her shoulder, and he smiled back. He was downright terrifying normally, but when he looked at Seraphia, his face softened, and I could finally understand what she saw in him.

Mostly.

She stopped in front of us. "I've found three entrances from the surface. Mac, Beatrix, and Quinn have gone to check one out."

I unrolled the map and held it out for her to look. "Same as these?"

Carrow pointed out the entrances that Ogden had shown us. Seraphia studied them, a frown on her face. "Two are different. One overlaps. Mine are both in churches. Hopefully, our friends can let us know about the first one soon."

"Great." I grinned. "Let's tell the shifters, and they can check the other one out."

"Do you need to keep looking?" Carrow asked. "Think you can find more?"

"I can keep looking while the others check those out," Seraphia said.

"Thank you." I smiled at her.

"Let me know if you need anything else, all right?"

"Sure thing."

Carrow and I said our goodbyes and left, heading back through town. The closer we got to our tower, the tenser my shoulders became. We had our backup from Lachlan, but my courtyard was the area where my attacker liked to hang out. I wouldn't be able to relax until we stepped through the door of the tower.

16

Lachlan

My brother seemed more lucid this time. As if sitting in the cell alone was giving him the space he needed to return to himself. His eyes were still black and his demeanor sullen, but I'd begun to take that stillness as a good sign, eerie though it might be.

At least he wasn't attacking. Perhaps he was retreating into himself in favor of acting out on the curse.

He'd taken one more truth potion—willingly this time, as if he wanted me to trust him—then said, "Go ahead."

"The girl they've got locked up—the one with the Dark Moon curse. Do you know her?"

"Know of her. She wasn't willing."

"Were you?"

"I—" His eyes cleared briefly, the whites reappearing. "I don't know."

Damn, I didn't like the sound of that. "Do you know what they're planning? Why they want Eve?"

"No. I might have once. I don't now."

What had happened to his mind? It was almost like it had scrambled. But if they were taking some wolves and forcing them to turn...

Then he might be innocent as well.

"How do they make a wolf turn?" Normally, it was a matter of time, genetics, and circumstance. Not something that could happen at the flick of a switch.

His brow furrowed, and he rubbed a hand over his face. Clearly, he was trying to remember, but it was proving difficult. "A spell, I think. Dark magic. So much dark magic."

"You could sense it?"

"It was everywhere. In the air, the walls." He shuddered.

Not a surprise. I'd felt it down there as well.

"Do they do this all underground in Clerkenwell?"

"No. That is new. Only been there a few times."

He was answering far more questions than he ever had before and much more willingly. Perhaps that willingness made the truth potion last longer. Or maybe he was answering because he wanted to.

"I've missed you, Garreth." The words came out before I could stop them, and I didn't regret them.

He stiffened, eyes clouding with confusion. The blackness overtook them once more, and he sat still and cold against the wall.

I leaned back, disappointed.

"I'll see you later, brother." I rose and left the cell. Despite the way it had ended, it hadn't gone too badly. Garreth was trying to fight the curse, I was sure of it.

"He's returning to himself more," I told Callum and Sophie. "But still, be wary."

They nodded, and I headed up the stairs. I had all the information I could get out of Garreth, and my security force had reported that Eve was safely back in her tower. Half a dozen of my shifters were out in London looking for the entrances to the tunnels.

I should go meet Eve.

Quickly, I headed across town, reaching the Shadow Guild tower in record time. I spotted no one on the rooftops as I went, and I wondered if her stalker had given up, assuming we might be coming back for him.

He wasn't wrong.

I didn't like the idea of Eve walking back into his lair, but at least we knew what we were going into.

At the door of her tower, I stopped and knocked. A rustling sounded from overhead, and I looked up to see Ralph hanging out the window. He stared at me, whiskers twitching.

A second raccoon leaned out of another window, and he looked at her, giving a brief hiss. Then he popped back inside.

The door swung open, revealing Eve on the other side. She stepped back to let me in, and I joined a small crowd in their main room. Carrow, Mac, and Beatrix were there, along with the four shifters I'd set as guards for Eve.

"Well?" Eve asked, walking back to take her place in a chair by the fire.

I stayed standing as I told them what I'd learned. None of it was unexpected, except the part about my brother possibly getting a little bit better.

"It will take my shifters a couple of hours to check the rest of the entrances," I said.

"Ours was a bust," Mac said.

"Until then—" Eve looked down at her phone, which had just vibrated. She read the message silently, then looked up. "Seraphia said she found one more promising entrance in the basement of a church in Clerkenwell. It was once a monastery."

"Let's check it out," Carrow said. "Better than twirling our thumbs here."

Eve jumped up. "I like it."

I frowned, not liking the idea of her going into danger like that.

She shot me a look. "Your disapproval is all over

your face. But you can't decide for me. In fact, you shouldn't even *want* to."

She was right. If I was trying to fight this mate bond, I shouldn't be giving into these protective urges—no matter how much ignoring them seemed to tear my soul out.

My hand itched to reach for my flask, but I resisted. The last thing I wanted was to show weakness here. Instead, I just nodded. "You are right. We will go with the appropriate backup and check it out."

The words felt like acid in my mouth, but they were the right ones. She was her own person, and I couldn't control her, no matter how much I wanted to wrap her up in cotton wool.

It was that very desire that scared the shit out of me, and it was good practice to resist it.

Eve grinned, then looked at her friends. "You guys want to come?"

"Wouldn't miss it." Mac hopped up, a broad grin on her face.

Beatrix nodded, her wild dark hair bouncing around her head, and Carrow just said, "Duh."

I looked at my shifters, and they nodded.

"Let's go then." I turned toward the door, looking forward to having this entire ordeal over with. I needed to get back to life as I knew it—quiet, cold, calm. Only then would I be able to maintain the focus necessary to be a proper alpha.

Eve

We reached the church in Clerkenwell an hour later. Evening was beginning to fall, and the shadows stretched long across the graveyard.

Lachlan joined me as we crossed toward the main entrance. "How are you? Were you able to rest?"

"Yes. A quick nap. And we slept some in our cell. I'm hanging in there."

"Good."

At the entrance to the church, his shifter guards held back. My friends crowded up to the front, of course. Mannerless heathens, the lot of them.

"Do you think it's empty?" Mac whispered.

"Could be, at this hour." I pushed open the heavy wooden door, stepping into the silent space.

My footsteps echoed on the marble floor as I entered. It was a simple church with a main aisle leading right up to the altar. Wooden benches stretched out on either side, and the arched ceiling was painted with angels.

"There's no one here," Lachlan said, tilting his head as if to use his shifter hearing. "Totally empty."

Some of London's churches had a policy of leaving

their doors open for worshipers at all hours, and I was grateful this was one of them.

"It's a lot bigger than this according to Seraphia's notes," Mac said, looking down at the paper in her hand. Seraphia had given it to her earlier when she'd opted to stay behind to continue researching entrances in case this didn't pan out. "Apparently it used to be a monastery in the medieval period. This was the main church, but the monks' quarters were in the basement."

"Did they use the tunnels, do you think?" Carrow asked.

"Yes," Mac said. "They would sneak over to have parties with the nuns."

"Parties?" I asked. "As in—"

"Yep," Mac said. "Sometimes parties that resulted in kids being born."

I whistled low. Scandalous monks and nuns. "That's unexpected."

"The Clerkenwell tunnels have quite a history." Mac pointed to the far corner of the church. "I think we can get to the basement through there."

We reached the stairs and headed down, single file with Lachlan in the lead and his shifters at the back. They were always silent and efficient when maneuvering themselves into the most protective positions, and there was no point fighting them on it. I appreciated it, in fact. The Shadow Guild could handle itself, but we were smart enough to take help when it was offered.

The bottom level was dark and musty. There were no electric lights, but a faint glow came from the church above, illuminating the space in shades of gray.

A narrow hall stretched through the basement, tiny rooms on either side.

"Do you think the monks once lived in them?" Beatrix whispered.

"Probably. Monks were really into asceticism, and this definitely qualifies." I peeked into a room and saw an ancient bed, so narrow that the sleeper would barely be able to roll over. I shivered and kept going.

"The air feels undisturbed," Lachlan said. "No recent scents that don't fit."

The shifters in the back rumbled their agreement, and we split up to check the rooms for a secret door. Lachlan stuck close by my side.

Near the back of the basement in the farthest room, I pulled back a faded old tapestry to reveal the wooden wall beneath. It looked normal, but I ran my hands along it, looking for any kind of secret latch or mechanism. We'd searched nearly the entire place now and were running out of options.

"Any luck?" Lachlan shone his torch on the door to give me a bit more light.

Beatrix joined us, standing at my side. She squinted at the wall, searching.

"Hold the light at a sharp angle," I said.

Lachlan moved, shining the light along the wood. It

caught on a slightly raised bit and cast a long shadow. I grinned and poked at the area, finding a slight indentation I hadn't been able to see before.

It depressed under my hand, creating a little handle. I dug my hand in and pulled. It inched open a bit, then stuck. I pulled harder. "This has to be it."

It creaked open, finally swinging free to reveal a dark hallway.

Filled with people.

My heart leapt into my throat.

Four large men crowded into the space, surrounding an older man in a cloak. The older man had his hands raised as he chanted a spell I didn't recognize.

Shock flashed on their faces as they saw us.

Lachlan called for his guards as he reached in and grabbed one of the men by the collar. He yanked him out and hurled him into the back of the room, where his guards caught him.

Two of the men charged us.

I grabbed a small stunner bomb from my wrist cuff and hurled it at them, hitting one dead in the chest. The thin glass exploded on impact, the highly concentrated solution creating a blast of force that knocked the man backward.

The other attacker lunged at Lachlan, who grabbed him and pulled him into our room.

The warlock chanted louder, and a massive cloud of black smoke exploded outward, obscuring our vision. I threw another potion bomb into the darkness, hoping to hit one of them.

Magic thrummed on the air, growing stronger and stronger.

Behind me, Lachlan fought the guard that he'd pulled out of the tunnel. I reached into the ether for my potion bag, withdrawing it and searching for a weapon.

A blast of magic hurled me backward, and I landed hard on the ground, my potions scattering out of my bag. I leapt upward, grabbing one of the bombs and aiming for the tunnel, which was still full of thick black smoke.

A figure reached out from the smoke and grabbed Beatrix, yanking her inside.

"No!" I raced forward, but too slowly.

The dark smoke solidified to form a solid wall of hard gray stone. It filled the entire tunnel, and panic made my head go fuzzy.

They have Beatrix.

I pounded at the stone, screaming.

Carrow raced up beside me. "What is it?"

"They got Beatrix." I pushed at the stone, shoving with all my might. "Lachlan, help me!"

He appeared next to me, pushing me aside and shoving at the stone. It didn't budge. Two of his guards joined him, bracing themselves against the door as they went red in the face from their effort.

"It's a solid rock," Lachlan said. "Not a door."

"No!" My skin went cold. "No!" Panic made the magic burn inside me. I raised my hand, reaching for the stone.

I had to move it. I'd moved other heavy things with my mind. Surely, I could move this.

But how?

I had no idea how that magic worked.

My eyes pricked with frustrated tears as I worked, trying to force the damned thing to move. Nothing happened.

I could feel it somehow—the sheer size of it was enormous. I wasn't strong enough to move it.

My breath came in panicked gasps, and I tried to force myself back into control. Carrow touched the stone, closing her eyes.

"Stop pushing," she told the men. "We can't move it. The earth has closed back in. It's impenetrable."

"But Beatrix..."

She turned to me. "We'll get her out."

"We have to." I shook my head. "The things they'll do to her..."

"We don't know what they'll do to her," Carrow said. "But they can't put her under the Dark Moon curse. She's not a shifter."

Carrow was right. Beatrix wasn't a shifter, even though she could turn into a raven. That magic was something different.

I'd worry about any of my friends, but Beatrix was

the newest to the magical world, and she was in there because of me. This had been my idea.

"They must have been closing off all the entrances," I said. "And we met them at exactly the wrong time."

"I think you're right." Lachlan inspected the stone. "Terrible timing. But now we know they have a warlock on the premises."

"They needed him for what they did to Garreth," I said. "Though I suppose the spell they used on Garreth was years ago."

"Either way, they've got one now," Lachlan said.

"We need to find another way in."

"My shifters are searching the other entrances right now," Lachlan said. "They'll find something."

I nodded, trying to keep the fear at bay. Carrow gripped my hand. "Let's get out of here and make our plan. We need to be efficient."

As we left, I looked back at the solid stone wall.

We'd get her out.

We had to.

17

Eve

Worry chilled my skin as we returned to the Shifter Guild tower.

They'd taken Beatrix.

I still couldn't believe it. She was trapped down there.

"It's going to be all right," Carrow said as we walked into the main room. "It's not your fault."

"Sure." Of course it was my fault.

I looked toward Lachlan, whose brow was set in concerned lines. We'd come back to the tower because his shifters would report back after their reconnaissance. Hopefully, one of them would find an entrance that hadn't been blocked.

But what if they didn't?

"We need a backup plan," I said to my friends, who'd all crowded around me. We stood in front of the massive hearth, the flames flickering merrily behind us. "Just in case the shifters don't find a way in."

"What's the plan?" Mac asked. "Draw them out?"

"How?" Carrow frowned. "You can't be thinking—"

"Bait." I nodded. "Me. That's who he wants."

"Absolutely not," Lachlan said.

"Afraid it's not up to you, buddy."

He looked as immovable as a mountain, his face implacable. I turned to my friends, determined to ignore him. We plotted our options as we waited to hear back from the shifters still out in the field.

One by one, they returned with news.

It was never good. All of the historic entrances had been blocked up. It was impossible to tell when they'd been cut off, but I had to assume it was recently. That damned warlock was probably making the rounds, shutting them all up.

Every second that passed made the fear stronger, until it took everything I had not to run out into London and try to draw my attacker to me.

That'd be unforgivably stupid, though. If we were even going to attempt my insane plan, everything would need to be perfect.

Finally, all of the shifters had returned with news.

And it was bad.

It got worse when the dwarves reported that they'd been unable to break through any of the blocked passages in the Below.

"We have to do it," I said.

"Eve—"

I cut Lachlan off. "I have a plan. I won't be going in alone. I'll have Garreth."

His jaw dropped. "My brother? The one who tried to murder us both."

"You said he was getting a bit better. More lucid."

"For incredibly brief periods, yes. But that doesn't mean he can sneak you in."

"He doesn't need to sneak me in. He just needs to take me to a place where the others will meet us. They'll bring me in."

"As a prisoner."

"A prisoner with a plan."

He dragged a hand through his hair. "This is madness. We can't guarantee that Garreth will stay lucid enough to even get you to the drop-off point. Or that he'll know of one."

"I can help him. He's been showing more lucidity, and there's a potion I can give him to help with that. It will hold off the madness a bit longer."

"Then you're trapped in there." Lachlan turned to my friends. "You're really not going to say anything about this insane plan?"

"She's got it worked out," Carrow said. "It's dangerous, but there's a plan."

"We use a double-sided portal charm," I said. "Carrow's mate Grey has one. I get abducted, and once I'm inside, I deploy the charm. You will have the other side of it, so you'll be able to come in and join me."

His eyebrows rose.

"Good plan, huh?"

He scowled. "Yes. For the most part."

"Don't give me any crap about how dangerous it is. It's my choice."

"Couldn't I wear a glamour and pretend to be my brother?" he said. "That way I can be the one to go in with you."

"You could if they didn't have that warlock. He might be able to see through it, then we're both screwed."

It was a good point, and he knew it. Warlocks had powerful magic, and one of their specialties was seeing through enchantments. The one we'd just encountered had gotten the drop on us in seconds, making it clear he was too powerful to test.

"This is our shot, Lachlan. You wouldn't leave a pack member behind."

"You're asking so much."

"We won't lose Garreth. You can put a tracking collar on him."

Lachlan turned to look at the shifter guards who stood behind him. His people had a stake in this, too, and he clearly wanted to know what they thought. Garreth had killed members of their pack. Technically, he *was* a member of their pack.

I'd seen Lachlan willing to make sweeping decisions without consulting his people, but something about this spoke of the fairness of a good alpha.

"What do you think?" Lachlan said.

The tallest guard—a man with sandy hair and a kind face—stepped forward. "You said there was a shifter girl in there? A captive?"

"Aye." Lachlan nodded. "She's been cursed, whether by fate or by the actions of those who kidnapped her, I don't know. She could be a lost cause."

"But she might not be," the man said. "We think it's worth risking Garreth to save her. He should be held accountable for his crimes, but that shouldn't come above protecting one of our own." He nodded at me. "Or one of their own either."

The others nodded.

I could see Lachlan's shoulders relax just slightly and realized that he was pleased with the assessment. It was what he'd wanted—to try to save Beatrix and the other girl—but he'd been wise to think about how his people would have felt about him letting Garreth out.

I knew he struggled with what his brother had become. He must dread what the future held in store for them.

Knowing Lachlan, he probably thought that he was

letting emotion get in the way. He wouldn't want to be biased.

Lachlan turned back to me. "We'll do it, but we must take all the precautions. I want to be in contact with you the entire time."

I nodded, gratitude welling within me. "Thank you. Truly."

He nodded, his jaw tight and his gaze worried.

I turned from him and looked at my friends. "Let's get everything we need."

Lachlan

Several hours later, after our forces had split up to collect the various supplies we'd need, we gathered back in the main room of my tower.

The members of the Shadow Guild entered together. My guards had followed Eve around town as she'd gathered her supplies, reporting back on her movements. Interestingly enough, I'd learned that she had a secret flat on the north side of town, a fact that I stored away for later.

I'd gone to Mordaca to collect another of her tracking collars for Garreth. It wasn't foolproof—none of this was—but I needed to take every precaution I could.

Eve and her gang of five stopped in front of me.

"Success?" I asked.

Eve nodded, and Carrow held up two small brilliant blue charms that glowed with an internal fire. "One for us, one for her. Grey will meet us there."

Grey, more formally known as the Devil of Darkvale, was Carrow's mate and the most powerful vampire in town. Hell, he was one of the most powerful people in town. It would be good to have him when this turned into a fight.

"There's a horrible demon uprising in the Underworld," Seraphia said. "Hades will get away as soon as he can. Hopefully, he'll be able to help."

"We've got this," Carrow said. "Anyway, can't have the demons running amok in the Underworld."

"No, it's...real bad." Seraphia grimaced.

Carrow handed Eve one of the charms. "Keep this where it can't be found. It gives off a faint magical signature, so if they frisk you, they might feel it, no matter how small it is."

"I'll keep it in the ether." She drew her bag and put the small stone into a little inner pocket in the bag.

"That will take time for you to retrieve." I frowned. "You'll need to be alone to get it out."

Carrow nodded. "Once you deploy the charm, it will take a minute or two for the link to form between the two. So don't do it until you have an undisturbed moment."

Worry turned in my gut. "That's too long."

"I'll manage," she said. "Trust me."

Trusting her wasn't my problem. It was fate and circumstance I didn't trust.

"It's going to be dark soon," Eve said. "That will be the perfect time to go in."

I frowned. "Why?"

It would be dark down in the tunnels no matter what, and I doubted they kept regular hours.

"Easier to sneak through the pub if it's closed."

That was a while off yet. There was something else she wasn't saying...

I debated asking her, but she was unlikely to share. And with so many other people around, it wasn't the time.

Later.

"Shall we go get Garreth?" she asked. "I have a potion that will help him keep his clarity of mind."

"Let's do it."

She turned to her friends. "Wait here?"

They nodded, and Eve turned back to me. "Let's go."

Together, we headed back through the tower and down the stairs. As we walked, I stared at Eve, hating every part of her plan but knowing it was a good one.

Halfway down the stairs, she halted, turning to look at me. The dim light cast dark shadows on her face, but her eyes shot fire. "Stop it, all right? I can feel your concern like a damned thousand-pound weight. You need to get that fated mate protectiveness under control. I know it's part of this whole bond thing, but it's driving me crazy. You don't even care that much about me, so rein it in."

All of the worry, the fear, bubbled to the surface inside me. I gripped her shoulders, pressing her against the wall. "It's not just the bond, damn it."

Wide eyed, she looked up at me. "It's not?"

"I care for you, damn it." As the words left my mouth, I knew I shouldn't have said them. They burned on the way out, the admission too much for my sanity.

"Like, *care* care?"

"I have no idea what that means." The beast inside me howled, hating that we were letting her walk into danger. It was just too much. "I didn't expect this. I shouldn't feel anything, much less this. But I do."

She drew in a ragged breath. "But nothing—"

"Nothing can come of this, I know. It's impossible for both of us. Worse than that, it's dangerous. You saw what my brother did while under the influence of the curse. I can't let that happen to me."

"I know. I don't want this any more than you do."

"I didn't say I didn't want it." More words that I shouldn't have said.

Surprise widened her eyes, and her lips parted. It was too much for me to take.

I leaned down and kissed her, pressing my lips to hers as the hunger tore me apart inside. All of this was impossible, but right now, I didn't care.

A tiny noise escaped her throat as she wrapped her arms around my neck and kissed me back. Heat flared within me, along with a desperate desire to be closer to her. To wrap her up and keep her with me forever.

It could never happen.

Which made the kiss all the sweeter.

Finally, I pulled away, forcing myself to remember what was at stake.

She drew in a ragged breath and looked up at me. "We can't."

"I know. Not ever, and especially not now." I stepped back, forcing myself under control. "Let's go get Garreth."

She nodded and followed me down the stairs. As I walked, I pulled the flask from my pack pocket and drank, feeling the welcome burn on my throat.

Thank fates she wore that charm around her neck. Her ability to hide her shifter nature kept most of our mate bond at bay, and I was so grateful I could fall to my knees with it.

Because if this was how I felt when I could barely feel the mate bond, what would happen if she took it off and I had to absorb the full force of it?

I shoved the thought to the back of my mind.

It wouldn't happen. I didn't have to worry about it.

We reached Garreth's cell a moment later. Callum and Sophie nodded at us.

"You are relieved," I said. "We're taking Garreth with us."

"Aye," Sophie said.

She and Callum headed up the stairs, and I turned to Eve. "You have the potion?"

She pulled her bag from the ether and withdrew a small vial full of green liquid. "I made a half dozen. He can't take them forever, but a few doses in a row won't hurt him."

"How long will it last?"

"Two or three hours. I'll give one to the girl when we get her so that she won't fight us."

"Assuming she wants to be rescued."

"Yeah, assuming that."

I took the vial and nodded. "What happens if he takes more than a few at a time?"

"He'll develop an immunity to it."

"Damn." It would have been incredible if he could have maintained his sanity with it. He'd be a ticking timebomb waiting for the moment he missed a dose, but the selfish part of me was willing to take the risk to have my brother back.

"I know," Eve said, and I had a feeling she did. "Let's do this.

I nodded and turned to the door, opening it.

When we walked in, Garreth was sitting on the floor

as usual, staring straight ahead. He looked up at us, eyes flashing briefly back to normal.

"Lachlan?" He frowned, confusion on his face.

"Hi, Garreth." I knelt by his side, hoping that his gaze would stay clear until he could take the potion. "Will you drink this? It'll help hold off the effects of the curse."

Interest flickered on his face, and he nodded, taking the potion from me. Quickly, he downed it.

Tension tightened my skin as I waited, watching to see if he appeared different. A moment later, he shuddered and dragged a hand over his face.

"That's a trip," he said.

"How do you feel?" Was my brother back? Could it be possible?"

"Like hell." Grief flashed on his face. "Tommy. Bill. Fates, did I do that?"

"Not you." I gripped his shoulder. "The curse."

"I still wielded the blade. The poison." He raised his hands and shuddered. "Fates, I'm a monster."

"Not anymore." I tugged him up. "We need your help."

He looked toward the cell door. "Out there? I don't think that's a good idea."

"You'll be fine," Eve said. "The potion will keep you sane for a few hours."

"And after?"

"You go back to the way you were."

He cursed again. "Is it worth it to take me out of here, then? Because... I can't control myself in that form."

"We've got something important at stake," I said.

"Someone," Eve corrected. "Two someones."

"More than that, when we count you," I said. "This all started because they're after you. They still are. You're at the heart of this. Your life is at risk as well."

Garreth blanched. "He's right. My original purpose was to kidnap you."

"But you went off the rails and started killing?" Eve asked.

"Yes. The curse overtook me, breaking all my loyalties. It was like this monster inside me, rising and forcing me to kill those I'd once loved."

Fates, it sounded terrible. "Were they the ones who cursed you?"

"They triggered it, yes. But the curse hits our line so strongly. You know that. They didn't expect it to happen, but it did. I went rogue before I could accomplish what they wanted me to." The guilt on his face made my heart clench.

"This is your chance to make good."

"I'll never make good on what I did."

He was right, and I couldn't argue the point. "It's a start."

He nodded. "What do you need me to do?"

"Get me in there," Eve said.

Garreth nodded again. "There are several entrances I can lead you to."

"They're all blocked," I said. "Do you know a way through?"

He frowned. "No. If the warlock has triggered the blocks, we can't get through without his permission."

"We expected as much," I said. "That's why you're going to pretend that you've escaped and accomplished your original goal."

"You want me to bring Eve to them?" He looked at me like I was crazy. "That's insane."

"I agree." He looked at Eve. "But she insists."

"I do," Eve said. "It's the only way. They have one of my best friends."

Garreth shrugged. "If you insist."

"Thank you. Let's go."

18

Eve

The walk to Clerkenwell was fraught with tension. Lachlan and Garreth led the way, and I followed with Carrow. The others kept up a little ways behind us.

Fortunately, it was late enough that the moon was high in the sky. That might give me some strength. Lachlan hadn't quite bought my reasons for wanting to go at night, but he'd gone along with it without asking for too many details, thank fates.

Carrow turned to look at me. "Your comms charm works?"

I pressed my fingertips to the earring I'd bought a few hours ago and felt the magic flare to life. "Testing."

My voice escaped the earring at Carrow's own ear,

and she grinned. The connection would be maintained until I turned it off, which I wasn't planning to do. Even better, the jewelry didn't emit a magical signature, so if they frisked me, they wouldn't think anything of it.

Hopefully.

I'd gone to the fae dress shop in town to purchase a tiny comms charm that had been crafted into a simple gold earring. Lachlan was smart to have wanted contact throughout the entire operation, and the fae were the masters of stealth.

With their charm and beauty, they made the perfect spies. So much so that they'd gained a reputation for it. There were several boutiques in town that specialized in clothing and accessories for those on covert missions. Dresses that repelled knives, bracelets that turned into daggers, and fancy comms charms were just the beginning.

I pulled a pair of enchanted cuffs out of my back pocket. They looked real, but I could break through them when I needed to. *Only* I could break them, however. If someone else yanked on them, they would stay strong.

A few blocks from the pub, Lachlan and Garreth stopped.

I looked behind us to see my friends and a select assortment of Lachlan's sifters stop on the block behind us. The portal charm wouldn't allow an endless number to come through, so he'd picked the best.

Garreth turned to us, his gaze on me. "Ready?"

I nodded.

"No guarantee I can protect you when we're in there," he said. "More likely than not, I can't."

"I've got it."

He nodded. I could feel Lachlan's gaze on me on me, but he didn't step forward.

For the best. It would be ridiculous, really. What was I expecting, a kiss goodbye?

Crazy.

"I'll deploy the charm as soon as I can," I said.

Lachlan nodded "We'll be ready. Leave your comms charm on."

"Yeah, of course."

Carrow snapped the cuffs on me, then gave me a tight hug. I waved at the rest of my friends, then joined Garreth. "Let's do this."

He nodded, then gave his brother a look. "When this potion wears off...put me down if you have to, all right?"

Lachlan grimaced, then nodded.

"I'm sorry," Garreth said.

Something unreadable flashed on Lachlan's face. "Not your fault."

"We both know that's not true." Garreth turned to me. "Come on."

I nodded and followed him, holding my hands so that my cuffs weren't readily visible unless someone knew to look closely. The last thing we needed was a human calling the police on us.

"You need to be careful," Garreth said as we walked toward the Bonnie Thistle. "These people are monsters."

"I know." I frowned up at him. "Do you know anything about why they want me, specifically?"

"No. I'd have told you if I did. What I've said already is everything I know."

I nodded, unsurprised.

It was about ten o'clock when we stepped into the pub. The crowd was smaller than it had been on my last visit, and no one paid us any mind as he headed to the back room.

A couple of guys sat at the booth that hid the door to the tunnels, and Garreth shot them a hard look. "Get out of here."

Their jaws dropped, and shock flashed in their eyes. Garreth was massive, and this wasn't the type of pub where bullies bossed around the rabble. All the same, the men scrambled up, grabbed their beers, and high-tailed it out of the room. Soon, we were alone.

Quickly, Garreth pulled the booth away from the wall. He looked at me. "Do you have a knife?"

I nodded and pulled a small flip knife from my pocket. "Here."

He took it and sliced his palm, letting the blood well to the surface before he pressed it to the wall. When he moved to hand it back to me, I shook my head. "Keep it. You need a weapon."

He looked at it, brow arched. "This little thing doesn't count. And I can shift if I need to."

"Fine." I took it back, watching the wall. "What's going to happen?"

"It will alert them that I'm here. Or at least, that's how it was supposed to work. Then, we're in."

"Excellent."

We waited, every second passing like an eternity.

"You hear all that?" I whispered to my comms charm.

"Yep." Carrow's voice carried through, nice and quiet.

A few moments later, the portal opened, revealing the narrow tunnel. I'd expected it to be empty.

Tragically, I was wrong.

A man crouched there, all massive muscles and scarred face, his suspicious gaze on us. Behind him, I could see more guards.

Shit, they weren't taking any chances.

The man eyed Garreth, suspicious. "Thought you were captured."

"Escaped. And got what I was sent for." He jerked on my arm, and I tried to look scared.

It wasn't hard. I *was* scared. No matter how good our plan, I was still walking into this craziness with just one guy as backup. And he could turn against me at any time.

The man climbed out, followed by another. They loomed over me, inspecting me.

"She's the one," Garreth said.

"Show us your palm."

My palm? I frowned.

He yanked on my cuffs, jerking my hand up. When he saw the glowing orb in the middle of my palm, he nodded, pleased. "She's the one."

Why the hell were they interested in me? What was it about my new power?

The guard patted down my pockets and any place that I might be able to hide a weapon. Finally, he stepped back. "She's clean."

Good thing we'd hidden the charm in the ether.

"Get in." He shoved me down toward the tunnel.

There were three men already inside it. They backed up so that I could join them, turning around so that they could crawl to the other end where the tunnel widened.

I followed them, with Garreth and the two other guards behind. They weren't taking any chances here. If I could get my friends in, we could outnumber them, but I couldn't deploy the charm until I had a minute alone.

A minute had never seemed so long.

The climb through the tunnel was dark and miserable. But it didn't get any better when we reached the wider part. One of the guards yanked me to my feet and dragged me behind him. Their strides were so long that I had to run to keep up.

We passed the prisons so quickly that I couldn't look inside to see if the woman was still there, and by the time we reached the main room with the machinery, I was panting.

It was still a mess from the chaos that I'd created last time, but the piles of broken steam machinery had been dragged to the side. Guards lined the walls—way too many of them—but I only had eyes for the guy who'd attacked me in Guild City.

He stood by his chair, appearing unwounded from our last run-in. His gaze was snake cold as he looked at me.

"Finally." Ice edged his voice, and he looked at Garreth, frowning. "He's been turned. Take him to the dungeons."

Shit.

I turned back to Garreth just in time to see one of the guards hit him over the head with a small bat, knocking him out. Fear iced my skin as they dragged his unconscious body away.

All around, I felt the eyes of the guards on me.

Too many. Way too many for me to get that minute I needed.

I looked up at the ceiling, seeking the moonlight.

Horror shot through me when I realized that they'd

blocked off the grates. The moon no longer shone through. Without access to the sky, I couldn't use my fae lightning. Nor could I call on my new powers.

I tried but felt almost nothing from the moon above.

The man's gaze followed me. "Yes. We blocked off the grates. You won't be able to use your power."

"What do you know about it?" I demanded. "Tell me."

"Not until he arrives."

"*He?* Who is he?" My heart raced. There was someone stronger than this man who wouldn't die? I'd stabbed him a dozen times and thrown thousands of pounds of steel on him, and he still looked fine.

"You'll know soon enough. Until then, you need to wait." He nodded at someone behind me.

I turned, but not soon enough.

Pain flared in my head, and darkness took me.

Lachlan

"What's happening?" I demanded. I'd been able to hear Eve's voice before, but now it was gone.

"Eve?" Carrow whispered, eyes wide. "Eve? Are you there?"

No response.

Carrow turned white. "They must have knocked her out."

"Not killed." They couldn't have killed her. They still needed her. Fear iced my spine.

"Yeah. They haven't gotten what they wanted." Carrow twisted her hands, clearly debating something. She turned to her friends, a question clearly in her eyes.

It was a question they recognized from the nods they gave her.

"What's going on?" I demanded. "What did they mean about the moon?"

Carrow turned back to me. "We didn't want to tell you. It's Eve's business. But…"

"But what? Spit it out."

"She can use the moon to fuel her magic, and it sounds like they've blocked it off. She said that there were grates in the ceiling that led up to the surface. It allowed the moonlight through, and she could use it."

"So they cut it off to weaken her."

"Yes. But your guild has the manpower to maybe find the part of London where those grates are. Maybe they could uncover them and give her the power she needs."

"You should have told me this before."

"Her secrets are her secrets."

"And now she's alone down there, seemingly unable to deploy the charm to get backup. And likely unconscious." I dragged a hand over my face and pulled my cell phone out. I made a quick call, getting everyone in the guild onto the task of scouring London. I did my best to give them directions, guessing at which part of London it could be in, but it was a long shot.

Still, we needed it to work. Fates, we needed anything to work at this point.

19

Eve

Slowly, I came to. My head ached like I'd been run over by a train, and the ground was hard beneath me. The air smelled damp and stale.

Where was I?

Groggily, I blinked.

It was dark around me, massive shapes towering overhead.

The world returned to me in a flash.

I was underneath London in the Clerkenwell tunnels. I'd been knocked out. My heart began to race as I tried to take in my surroundings without moving.

I lay at the edge of the huge room, right in front of a

row of giant steam machinery that I hadn't broken last time I'd been here. It towered overhead.

Across the room, the leader spoke to some of his guards. There were others scattered around the room, keeping watch, but none seemed to have their eyes on me right now. No doubt they still thought I was unconscious.

Eve.

Ralph's voice sounded in my head.

"Where are you?" I whispered.

Behind you. In the shadows of the machinery.

He was probably five feet behind me then. Thank fates they'd tossed me over here. With the moon covered and my wrists bound with magicuffs, they probably doubted I could do anything.

Idiots.

"You need to deploy the portal charm." Only he could sneak away long enough to do it.

How?

"It's in my bag." Carefully, I called it from the ether. It appeared at my side, lying crumpled on the floor. "Sneak up beside me and drag it back there."

I got a key. To all the cells. Beatrix is okay.

"Really?" Hope flared in my chest. "Leave it with me."

All right.

I searched the room, making sure none of the guards were watching. "Now, Ralph."

He scurried up beside me, a little shadow as he left the key at my side and dragged the bag back. I grabbed the key, tucking it into my palm.

"Take it somewhere that no one will see you," I whispered. "Then deploy it."

I'll leave the potion bag for you back here in case you need it. But I'm taking some bombs.

"Fine." Of course he'd jump on that opportunity.

As he rustled around in the bag, I watched the room. They really weren't looking at me. And this might be my only chance to rescue Beatrix and Gareth. And the woman.

I had to take it.

I couldn't attack until my friends were here anyway, so this was the best option.

I've got the portal charm. I'm out of here.

I waited a minute to make sure the coast was clear, then scrambled up and disappeared behind the tower of machinery, snatching up my bag as I went. Once I was hidden between the wall and the tower of defunct steam engines, I yanked my wrists apart, separating the cuffs that bound me.

Quickly, I raced along the back wall, headed toward the cells. If only I had the invisibility potion that I'd given Ralph back at the library in Magic Side.

But it had been useful in saving his furry hide back there, and I wouldn't trade that.

I gripped a sleeper bomb in my hand as I called

upon my wings and launched myself into the air. I stayed fairly low to the ground so that I could hide behind the bulk of the machinery, but high enough that I wasn't within anyone's eye level. My sleeper bombs were the most subtle of my arsenal, and that was what I needed right now.

By the grace of fate, I ran into no issues on my way to the cells. There was a guard standing in front of one of them—had to be Garreth's—and his eyes widened when he saw me.

I chucked the bomb at him, and the glass exploded silently against his chest. His eyes rolled back in his head, and he slumped against the wall.

Quickly, I raced to the cell door and peered through the narrow slats in the window, spotting Beatrix.

Her face brightened, and she leapt up. "Eve!"

I fumbled with the key, happiness flaring within me. "I've got the key. Hang on."

Seconds later, I heard the lock snick, yanked the door open and she rushed out, hugging me tight.

"Thank fates you're okay."

"Thank you for coming for me."

"To quote Carrow, duh."

She pulled back and grinned. "I saw them bring Lachlan's brother in."

"Good. We need to get him out. I have a potion that will help keep him sane."

She pointed to a cell next to hers. "I think it's that one."

I hurried to it and looked through the bars.

Garreth sat against the wall, his eyes black.

Damn it.

"Garreth," I whispered, digging around in my bag for a dose of the potion that would give him some sanity. I just had to convince him to take it. "It's me, Eve."

His gaze flicked to me, briefly returning to normal. "Eve? Are you all right?"

"Come here." I gestured him forward. "I've got a potion for you."

"Same one that keeps me sane?" His eyes flickered black, and he shook his head hard, as if trying to fight off the curse.

"Yeah."

He jumped up and came to the door. I made sure his eyes were normal before handing the potion over to him. Quickly, he drank it.

"Thank you."

"Yeah." I unlocked the cell door and let him out, then went to the next one.

The girl was still there, thank fates. She lay on the ground, her black eyes staring at the ceiling.

Garreth joined me, his gaze alert as he kept watch for guards. "What's the status on backup?"

"Ralph is getting them. I think they should be here any moment."

"Good." He looked at the woman in the cell. "Will your potion help her, too?"

"You'll have to force her to take it, maybe, but yes."

He nodded. "Give it to me."

I handed him the potion and unlocked the cell door, swinging it open. Beatrix and I stepped aside.

The woman jerked upright, but Garreth was fast. He raced inside and grabbed her, using his bulk to subdue her while he dumped the potion down her throat. As soon as she swallowed, he moved back, his hands raised. "We're here to help you."

She rubbed her face, her eyes returning to a shade of blue that was the color of a summer sky. "What happened to me?"

"You were kidnapped." I dug into my bag, retrieving the little gadget that Ogden the dwarf had given me. I pulled it out and handed it to her. "Use this. It will take you to the surface where some friends are waiting for you."

"Escape?" She looked at the device, hope in her eyes.

"Yes." I looked at Garreth. "You can take her."

"No way in hell I'm leaving you alone down here."

There would be no budging him on that point, it was clear.

"You know I'm not leaving you," Beatrix said.

The woman's gaze shadowed. "But what about the bastards that did this to me?"

"We're going to try to stop them."

Her face hardened. "I want a piece of them."

I couldn't blame her. I'd feel the same. But... "It's too dangerous."

"Let me decide that for myself, all right?"

"Fair point." It's what I'd wanted from Lachlan, after all. "You can come with us if you want."

She climbed to her feet. "I will."

"Do you know what they have planned?" I asked.

"No. Not exactly. Something to do with the Dark Moon curse, but I don't know what. It's got to be bad, though."

Understatement of the century. "Yeah. Come on, let's go."

I gave them each a handful of potion bombs, but they were likely to shift in the event of a fight. Beatrix would definitely use them, though. Properly armed, the four of us made our way quickly back to the main room, and I prayed that our backup had arrived.

When we reached the cavernous space, I didn't spot anyone from our side.

"This way," I whispered, leading them to a hiding spot behind the machinery.

As soon as we'd taken up our space, someone shouted.

"She's gone!"

Six guards ran toward the spot where they'd put my body. I'd only been gone a few minutes, but I was lucky they hadn't noticed sooner.

"Look for her!" the leader shouted. "He's almost here!"

There was a note of fear in his voice that sent a shiver down my spine.

"He's talking about the Maker," Garreth said.

Damn, if *he* was scared of the Maker and they were on the same side, then I sure as hell was.

The guards split up, searching the cavern. It would be only minutes before they found us.

Come on, backup.

A cloud of black smoke appeared in the middle of the cavern, bursting to life with a boom. When it dissipated, a figure stood there. His form was hazy and pitch black, as if he were made of the smoke itself. I squinted. I could see a solid core to him, though.

Was he some kind of demon?

Or was this a spell?

He turned in a circle, his voice booming. "Where is she?"

"She's here," my attacker said.

"She is." The Maker turned right toward me, reaching out a smoky hand.

A force grabbed me around the neck and pulled me forward. My insides turned to ice, and I thrashed against his hold, my wings beating as I tried to tear myself away.

He dragged me right up to him, so close that I could see that his eyes were made of flame. His face didn't have clear features like a normal person's. Instead, he looked like a solid core of darkness surrounded by black smoke. His magic reeked of death and decay, tasted like salt, and felt like the lick of fire.

"Who are you?" I gasped.

"You're the one?" He made a disgusted noise. "So unimpressive."

"The one, what?" I clutched one of my potion bombs by my side. I should throw it, but not until backup arrived. And I wanted whatever answers he had for me.

"I'd hoped for more." He shook me like a doll.

I thrashed against him, trying to break free.

"So weak," he said. "I'm not sure you'll do for my plan, but you're all I've got."

"What plan?" My words barely choked out past my throat. His grip felt tighter and tighter with every second.

A shout sounded from behind me, followed by more. Guards scattered, and out of the corner of my vision, I spotted three wolves, including a massive black one.

Lachlan.

Backup was here.

Thank fates.

The distraction caught the attention of the Maker, and I managed to hurl a potion bomb right at his chest. It exploded, the force of it blowing him backward. He released my neck, and I fell to the ground, landing hard before rolling away and leaping to my feet.

All around, the battle raged. Lachlan fought three of the guards while in his wolf form, blood spraying as he tore at flesh and bone. In the distance, Seraphia grabbed two of the guards with her vines, throwing them into the air.

Quinn, a panther, raced across the room, headed for the man who had attacked me in Guild City. Mac followed, a short sword in her hand. Carrow and Beatrix wielded potion bombs, and I spotted the Devil in the corner, tearing the head off one of the guards.

The Maker rose, turning to me.

I faced him, raising another one of my potion bombs.

"They can't stop me," he said. "My forces can't be killed."

To my horror, I realized that he was right. Behind him, Lachlan had torn the throat out of one of the guards. His neck looked like ground meat, blood soaking his front, and yet still, he fought.

Just like with my original attacker, back in the courtyard in front of my tower. It hadn't mattered that I'd stabbed him over a dozen times. He'd just kept going.

How were we going to defeat the unkillable?

All around, our forces were taking a beating. They'd had the upper hand at first, but now...

We were going to have to tear them all apart. Or bury them beneath machinery, like I'd first done.

Above me, light began to shine.

I looked up, hope flaring.

The metal plates that had covered the grates were being pushed aside. Moonlight flowed in, shining on my face with a brilliant warmth.

Power shot through my veins, and I gasped. It filled me with strength. Suddenly, I could feel the heavy objects all around me. The way I could sense them was like a crazy form of echo location.

I raised my hand, my palm burning, and let the moonlight power my gift. I pulled the pieces of heavy metal from the ground, slamming them into our attackers. It was hard, though. I didn't have the control I needed to avoid hitting my friends, and my efforts only made a dent in the fight.

All around, wolves and other shifters were being injured. Mac took a punch to the face that sent her reeling, and Beatrix ended up on the wrong end of a sword, the metal slicing into her thigh. She staggered away, hurling a potion bomb at her attacker. He went down, but then so did she, the wound too much.

Panic flared inside me. The other side looked worse with every minute that passed, more and more wounds appearing on their bodies, but they never stopped fighting.

The Maker roared and approached me, his stride unwavering as his gaze burned with flame.

I turned my attention to him, picking up a massive iron pipe with my magic and hurling it at him. It slammed into his chest, slowing him, but he didn't stop. I hurled another at him, but it barely slowed him.

Panicked, I stepped backward, fear icing my veins.

Soon, he was only feet from me.

"I've searched for you for years," he growled. "Finally, I've found you."

"For what?" I demanded. "Tell me!"

"You and I are alike, you know. Two halves of a whole."

I looked at him, horrified. "Alike? Never."

"Oh, you have no idea. That moon power of yours isn't random. And finally, it is time. We will control the curse."

He reached out with a shadowy hand and yanked my necklace away from my throat. His claws raked me, a slice of pain that burned like fire. It felt like it tore at my very soul, and I screamed.

As soon as the necklace was gone, it felt like a weight had been lifted off my soul.

The moon's energy surged into me, lighting me up like a live wire. My entire body vibrated, and my breath came short. I looked up at the moon, drawing its strength into me.

I'd never felt like this before.

Surely, no one had ever felt like this before. The sheer force of the power threatened to rip me apart. Every atom in my body felt like it wanted to tear away from the one next to it.

I had to do something with this energy—had to dissipate it.

Use it against my enemies.

It was the only way.

I drew in a ragged breath, trying to keep from going to my knees. I raised my hand and directed it at the Maker. The energy exploded out of me. Brilliant white light lit the room. It shot into my attacker, driving him backward. He disappeared in a flash of black and white light, an impossible light show that reeked of death.

I went to my knees, nearly blacked out from the pain. In my peripheral vision, I could see the other fighters still standing. The Maker's unkillable forces were still here.

I gasped, turning my attention to them. The crazy energy still vibrated through me, demanding to be released. I focused, trying to find them all, then unleashed my power directly at them. I had no idea what I was really doing—I just prayed it would work.

All around, the Maker's fighters fell. Beams of my brilliant white light slammed into them, driving them against the walls and piles of machinery. They lay still, silent.

Agony seared me, the force of the transition knocking me onto my back.

My head slammed into the ground, and I blacked out.

20

Lachlan

"Eve! Eve, wake up!" I shook her shoulders gently, trying to rouse her. Fear iced my spine as I took in her pale, glowing face.

Please be okay.

When her charm had been torn from her neck, I'd felt it like a punch to the gut. Our bond had exploded to life, stronger than ever. My soul had felt pulled to hers, the intensity of it stunning.

The beast had woken inside me, growling *mine*.

Finally, she managed to pry her eyes open. "What happened?"

Relief rushed through me. "Are you all right?"

"I'm fine." Wincing, she sat up.

"Um, not sure you are," Carrow said from my side.

I hadn't even realized she was there. All of her friends surrounded us, but in my fear, they'd been invisible to me.

"What?" Eve asked.

"You're glowing," Carrow said.

And she was. Her skin had a faint luminescence, like that of the moon. It had been brighter when the charm had first been torn away, but it was still distinctly noticeable.

She looked down at her hand, frowning. "What the hell?"

"Your whole body is glowing," I said. "But it's fading a bit."

She blinked, her gaze still fuzzy, and looked as though she might pass out again. Weakly, she asked, "Did we win at least?"

"For now," I said. "You took out the minions, but the leader disappeared. He'll be back though. Someone with that much rage won't quit."

"He's so powerful." She shivered, eyes stark. "Did he know I'd become so powerful when he yanked the necklace off?"

"It looked intentional." The charm must have been suppressing her new magic, and with it gone, her new power went out of control.

She looked around. "Where's Garreth?"

Shite.

In my panic over Eve, I'd forgotten about Garreth. He'd been at the front of my mind until she'd been wounded. I looked up, searching for him. I spotted every single one of my pack, except for him.

No.

On the ground, Eve swayed, her eyes fluttering shut. I reached for her, gripping her shoulders to lower her back down. Worry shot through me. "Lie still."

"Garreth?" she asked.

I swallowed hard, dread rising inside me. "Garreth is gone."

Eve

Sometime later, I woke in my bed. The pain was gone, but I felt weird.

At my bedside, Mac bolted upright. She'd been snoozing, and her hair was a wild mess of gold around her head. "How do you feel?"

"Fine." I sat up. "What time is it?

"More like what day."

"Huh?" I rubbed at my face, trying to wake up fully.

"You've been out cold for three days."

"No way."

"Way. Lachlan hasn't left our sitting room since we brought you back here. It was all we could do to keep him from barging in here."

"Thank you for trying." I slumped back against the headboard. "I wouldn't have wanted to wake up to him hovering over me right now. I must smell like a football team."

"He might be into that."

I laughed, then sobered at the thought of Lachlan's brother. "What about Garreth?"

"We haven't found him yet. Or the woman."

"Shit. They wanted to fight on our side."

"And they did. Until the potion you gave them wore off. They disappeared."

"I gave them Ogden's device to help them find the surface. They were supposed to go to the guards who waited for them."

"I doubt they went that way."

"Same." Shit, shit, shit. We'd lost them both, and they were cursed. "Is everyone else okay?"

"Besides some ugly wounds, yeah. Recovering fine."

"Thank fates."

"But you... Do you remember anything?"

I searched my mind. "I glowed." I looked down at my hand. "It stopped."

"And thank fates it did. We had no idea what that

was. But that shadowy guy took your necklace. You're a shifter again."

I felt for my ears, wincing when I realized they were no longer pointed. "Shit, Lachlan. He can feel the bond."

Now that I was fully awake, I could feel it, too. It tugged me toward him, making my heart race. "I need to get to my secret workshop. I have to make another."

"You can sneak out the window while I hold him off."

I can come.

Ralph jumped up onto the foot of the bed.

"Thanks, Ralph." Aching, I climbed out of the bed.

Ralph hurried to the window and jumped up onto the sill, pushing it open. *Coast is clear.*

"I'll make sure Lachlan is distracted," Mac said. "Just give me a few minutes."

I nodded, hurrying to my dresser to put on jeans and a shirt, then finishing the outfit off with boots. A few minutes later, Ralph and I scrambled down the tree outside my window. I already missed my damned wings.

As quickly as we could, we made our way across town. Fortunately, we made it to my workshop without trouble, and it didn't take me long to create the potion. With every minute I worked, my mind raced, going over what had happened.

I still had no idea what the Maker had meant, but something had changed in me. Wild new powers had appeared, and he'd said something about me being like him.

Not good.

The mere idea terrified me. I didn't want to be a monster like him.

We'd gotten rid of the problem of my attacker and saved Beatrix, but it felt like I'd opened an even bigger can of worms.

I'd focus on it later.

Right now, I needed to get this charm made. It was the only thing that stood between me and Lachlan, our main line of defense against the bond that we both fought because the potion Mordaca had given him was losing its effectiveness.

When my potion was done, I found another charm necklace. It was the last one in my stash, and I'd need to buy some more, given how my luck was going. I dipped it in the potion, watching with satisfaction as the glow dimmed.

It was done.

I put it around my neck, waiting for the rush of magic.

But nothing happened.

I frowned.

I'd made the potion correctly.

You still look like you. Ralph said. *No pointed ears. And you're kind of glowing.*

"Glowing?" I looked toward the mirror on the wall, spotting the faint glow to my skin. "Shit."

As I watched, the charm crumbled into dust.

Shock drove the breath from my lungs.

It was the transition.

That's what my attacker said. I had to go through a transition. That must have been what had happened when the white light had exploded out of me.

I swallowed hard. Holy fates, he was right. Something about the transition—whatever it had been—was devouring the magic that I used to hide myself as fae.

I blinked, staring at my stunned reflection. "I can't hide as fae anymore." I looked at Ralph. "What will I do?"

He grimaced, twisting his little paws. *I don't know.*

More importantly, what would Lachlan do?

I didn't need to hide my species anymore. The truth was out about me. Sure, I liked my fae powers, but the main reason I'd returned to wearing the charm was to suppress the bond between me and Lachlan.

Now that I couldn't hide from it...

Holy fates.

"I need to go see Liora," I said. Surely the master potion maker would know a solution. She'd known how to make the first potion. She'd know how to make another.

But even as I thought it, I knew it was impossible. The memory of the charm disintegrating around my neck made that clear enough. I'd never seen a magic so strong.

"I'll just need to avoid Lachlan," I said, panic making my mind buzz. "That's all. Easy."

Um—

"Yeah. I know it's not a great plan, but it's what I've got. Now come on, we need to sneak back into my tower." I turned and went to the door, swinging it open.

On the other side, Lachlan stood, his gaze dark with concern. The bond between us pulled so hard that it made me gasp.

"Eve." He gripped my shoulders. "The bond. It's too powerful."

"Yeah. Um...." My heartrate rocketed.

"You need to create another one of those charms." His eyes blazed with heat. "I can't feel like this."

I gasped, feeling the tug toward him. The desire blooming inside. Oh fates, how were we going to get out of this?

"I can't." I licked my lips, and his gaze dropped to them. "I can't make another. It's impossible."

"Eve." He drew in a shuddery breath, his eyes flashing black.

It was only for a second, but it was clear as day.

The Dark Moon curse.

Fear pierced me. "Lachlan, your eyes."

"I know." He shuddered. "You need to run, Eve. Run."

I drew back from him, my skin icy. Without a backward glance, I slipped around his broad frame and ran from the building like my life depended on it. And maybe it did.

I hope you enjoyed *Wild Hunt!* Book three, *Pack of Lies*, will be here in early April. Click here to get it. If you liked the character Nevaeh Cross, her series is out now. Click here to get book 1, Wicked Wish.

THANK YOU FOR READING!

I hope you enjoyed reading this book as much as I enjoyed writing it. Reviews are *so* helpful to authors. I really appreciate all reviews, both positive and negative. If you want to leave one, you can do so at Amazon or GoodReads.

ACKNOWLEDGMENTS

Thank you, Ben, for everything. There would be no books without you.

Thank you to Jena O'Connor and Lexi George for your excellent editing. The book is immensely better because of you! Thank you to Susie Johnson and Jenna Ossip-Klein for the excellent typo hunting.

Thank you to my amazing narrator Laurel Schroeder for bringing the character's voices to life.

Thank you to Orina Kafe for the beautiful cover art and Chris Sim for the guild crests.

AUTHOR'S NOTE

Hey there! I hope you enjoyed *Wild Hunt*. If you've read the author's note for *Darkest Wish*, you may be familiar with the fact that much of Guild City is based upon Sighișoara in Transylvania, the birthplace of Vlad the Impaler (inspiration for The Devil of Darkvale, the hero of The Rebel series).

This book delves a little bit deeper into the history of London, thanks to my author friend C.N. Crawford. She suggested using the tunnels of Clerkenwell for one of my story ideas, and it was perfect.

The tunnels are a series of underground passages beneath the Clerkenwell neighborhood. The prison that played a role in the book is based upon the real Clerkenwell House of Detention, an underground prison built in 1847. The river that Eve and Lachlan cross in the underground is the Fleet River, one of London's underground rivers. It runs at the boundary of Clerkenwell.

In the medieval period, the tunnels were said to be used by monks paying a visit to the nuns nearby. In this case, the entrance to the tunnels was in a monastery, which I tried to show in the book. However, I played a bit fast and lose with history and made the tunnels also accessible by a priest hole. There isn't a known example of a priesthood accessing the tunnels (they were used for a different purpose) but they were so cool that I wanted to add it in. In reality, priest holes were used to hide Catholic priests during the 16th century when they were being persecuted for their religion.

That's it for the history in this book. Thank you for reading, and I hope you stick around with Eve and Lachlan to find out more.

ABOUT LINSEY

Before becoming a writer, Linsey Hall was a nautical archaeologist who studied shipwrecks from Hawaii and the Yukon to the UK and the Mediterranean. She credits fantasy and historical romances with her love of history and her career as an archaeologist. After a decade of tromping around the globe in search of old bits of stuff that people left lying about, she settled down and started penning her own romance novels. Her Dragon's Gift series draws upon her love of history and the paranormal elements that she can't help but include.

COPYRIGHT

Printed in Great Britain
by Amazon